Betrayed in Taiwan
Sharolyn Richards

Western Skies Press, LLC

Copyright © 2024 Western Skies Press, LLC

All rights reserved.

No part of this publication may be reproduced, distributed, or transmitted in any form or by any means, including photocopying, recording, or other electronic or mechanical methods, without the prior written permission of the publisher and author, except as permitted by U.S. copyright law. For permission or requests, contact westernskiespress@gmail.com

The story, all names, characters, and incidents portrayed in this production are fictitious. No identification with actual persons (living or deceased) is intended or should be inferred.

Book Cover by Mikaela Fisher

1st edition 2024

Acknowledgements

Any acknowledgment for any book I write has to start with a big thank you to my husband and children for always supporting and believing in me.

A big thank you to my writing peers in my writing group who tell me the hard things and continue to encourage me and answer my questions.

I also have to thank the wonderful editors at Cookie Lynn Publishing Services. They took a rough story and helped me create the work that you now hold. Publishing a book has been a long time in coming, and I'm grateful the editors were patient with my questions as I found the story I truly wanted to tell.

And thanks to you for taking the time to read the words I worked so hard to put to paper.

To my children. Always follow your dreams no matter how impossible they seem.

Chapter 1

I stood with my back erect, and my face like stone as the people who had attended the graveside service left the cemetery. My full make-up look was just as Mom would have liked, and holding back tears preserved that look. Dad would have been proud of my hiding emotion throughout the service. Grace Little, my neighbor, hung back until the last person had left. Then she walked toward me, a frown on her wrinkled face, her short gray bobbed hair windblown, and her arms stretched out wide.

A sob cracked my stoic façade, and I put my face into my hands as her arms encircled me. I took deep breaths and wiped at the tears that had escaped. *Hold it together. For Dad's sake.*

Grace had lived next door as long as I could remember. Grace's embrace was strong despite her age. When I was younger, her height and direct way of talking scared me, but she had become one of my dearest friends.

"I am so sorry, Alia." Grace cleared her throat. "I loved your parents dearly. First, your mom when you were only a teenager, and now your father."

I bobbed my head, unable to say anything. My grief held me tight beneath Grace's gentle pats against my back. I resented the fact that I couldn't let everyone know how much I hurt. They guessed, I was sure, but my parents had raised me to hide my pain from the outside world. That was what family was for. But they never prepared me for when that family was no longer there.

"Come home with me," Grace murmured.

I shook my head. "I want some time alone with them."

Grace hesitated, studying me. "Okay."

I watched her walk away, fighting the urge to call her back. She was one of the last people I could trust enough to help me—well, her and Luke Douglas. I didn't want to burden them with my problems. I waited until her car disappeared before I slumped to the ground. I just stared at the names of my parents on the headstone, wondering how my life had changed so completely. When my mom died, I at least had my dad to turn to. I wasn't sure who I should let comfort me now. Most likely, it would be Luke.

My chest clutched my heart, squeezing harder and harder until I couldn't breathe. I gasped as tears flowed down my cheeks.

They were gone. Fear simmered below my grief. Ever since Mom died, I had allowed Dad to make every major decision in my life knowing I might make the wrong choice. Being the only child, he had been content to lead me along. The fact was, I didn't trust myself to make the decisions I needed to make. Maybe if I stayed here next to their graves long enough, their spirits would appear and tell me what I needed to do.

My fingers dug into the soft dirt around my father's grave, grasping for something to pull me out of this new reality. My fingertips found the hardened dirt of Mom's grave reminding me that Dad was all I had until last week. I couldn't survive without him.

"Why didn't you take me with you, Dad?" I whispered, longing to feel my mom's gentle embrace and my father's strong hand on my back.

It was a ridiculous question. I would be lying next to him if I had gone to Baja with him, but maybe if I had been there, Dad wouldn't have gone scuba diving. It was wishful thinking that my presence would have changed anything. Dad always did what he felt he needed to do. He had told me how important this trip was. Maybe he sensed danger and that is why he insisted I stay home. My safety had been paramount in every decision. My friends had told me he was overbearing, and sometimes I resented his rules. I would have never done anything against his wishes, though.

"Alia?"

I whirled around to face a young man in a UCONN sweatshirt. He stood a few feet away; his blond hair flitted across his forehead in the cold winter breeze.

His eyes were so dark they almost looked black. Those eyes studied me, and his mouth turned in a frown.

"Yes?" I stood. This man didn't look familiar. How did he know my name?

He jutted his chin toward my parents' gravestone. "You know why your father died, don't you?"

I shook my head, thinking back to when I looked at his body. His closed eyes, perfectly pressed clothes, and combed hair hadn't given me any clues about his death. The police said he died in a scuba accident, probably drowned somehow.

"You should have kept him home. Then he wouldn't have died."

I clenched my hands into fists. How dare he make it sound like I had anything to do with what happened in Baja? It was ridiculous. It almost sounded like his death wasn't an accident. I covered my mouth with my hand as I fought a small wave of nausea. The police who had come to inform me about his death hadn't said anything like that. I turned my back on him, hoping that would make him magically disappear.

"Alia. What will happen now that your father is gone? What will happen to his company?"

So that is how he knew me. I almost asked him if he worked for Dad, but something about his eyes stopped me. A flit of his pupils made me pause. A shiver ran up my back.

"I'm sure my dad had everything taken care of how he wanted." Luke would have never let the subject drop until everything was legally in place.

Something flashed in this man's eyes, and they grew darker, hate evident in their depths.

I scanned the cemetery, hoping someone was around. A funeral director stepped through the gate, and I sighed. The stranger followed my gaze. He turned without another word and walked away.

Confusion whirled in my mind. Fear clenched my stomach, and grief tore at my heart. The combination of all I was feeling made me want to crumble to the ground. I forced my emotions down long enough to talk with the funeral director and then climbed into my car.

I hiccupped as I held back tears and pushed what the stranger had said out of my mind. But the more I tried not to think about it, the more it made its way into my thoughts. I pressed my hands into my eyes to block it out. *He's wrong.* I told myself. *He's after the company. There is nothing you could have done to save him.*

I should have asked him who he was. He probably wouldn't have told me anyway.

That night I sat, staring at the family picture on the wall. I hadn't moved since coming home from the cemetery. Someone knocked on the door, but I ignored it. It was probably Grace checking on me, but I didn't want to face anyone. I wanted to wallow in my misery.

My phone rang, and my breath caught in my throat. Luke Douglas's name flashed on the screen.

"Hello." My voice was barely a whisper, so I cleared my throat. "Hello?"

"Alia. How are you?"

The compassion in his voice sent tears flowing anew down my cheeks. "Not good."

Luke was practically my uncle, though not through blood ties.

"I'm sorry I couldn't stay for the graveside service. I had work to do to start implementing your father's will."

"So, he did have one?" I asked, even though I knew the answer.

"What kind of lawyer would I be if I didn't make sure my best friend had a will?"

I chuckled slightly, which surprised me. I didn't think I had any happiness left in my heart.

"Listen, Alia. I'm sorry to call you today, but I really need to speak to you. Could you come to my office?"

I cringed. "It's almost 6:30. Why are you still at work?"

"This is important. I can come to your house if you'd prefer."

I hesitated while I scanned the front room. The house wasn't a mess, mostly because I had cleaned furiously the day I expected Dad, only to find out he wouldn't be coming.

"Yeah. Come here."

"I'll be there in twenty minutes."

I forced myself to my bathroom and stared in the mirror. Strands of my blond hair fell out of the elegant French twist I had worn to the funeral to appear put together. I took it out, and it flopped to my waist. I ran a brush through it until my head tingled. My eyes were puffy and bloodshot, and my head throbbed. I did my best to fix my makeup and swallowed a few pain relievers, wishing they would numb the pain in my heart as well as my headache. Satisfied that I had made myself as presentable as possible, I left the bathroom.

The doorbell rang as I reentered the front room.

I opened the door. I leaned into Luke and wrapped my arms around his portly midsection. Luke squeezed my shoulders.

His dark brown eyes were full of compassion as he stepped back to examine me. "I'm sorry I have to bother you today, but it's urgent."

He followed me to the couch and pulled out several documents. While he booted up his computer, he jumped straight into the will.

My mouth dropped open when he pointed at the amount I was inheriting. "Are you sure?"

His lips twitched slightly, and he nodded.

"How did I not know?"

"This house is yours, free and clear. Your dad left you no debts, but I'm worried someone will try to get into his bank accounts through the company to steal most of that."

"Why would they do that?" I asked.

Luke's eyes shifted from mine, and he busied himself with the computer. "Your father was vague, but he mentioned he thought the president of the company he was doing contracted work for, Frank Barlow, was up to no good. I would guess embezzlement."

"Why was my father doing work for someone like that?"

Luke put his hand on my shoulder. "I don't know all that was going on, but believe me, your father was an honest, trustworthy man."

"Some guy came to me at the cemetery and told me I should have kept him home," I whispered, forcing the words out. Repeating it made it feel more real. "He made it sound like it was my fault."

Luke's mouth tightened. "None of this was your fault. What did the guy look like?"

"About my age, maybe a little older. Shaggy blond hair. A little taller than me. Dark, threatening eyes and wearing a UCONN hoodie." I almost shrugged to make it seem like I didn't believe him, but Luke would see right through me. I leaned forward to support my chin in my hands.

Luke took a deep breath. "We should move the money from the business account set aside for personal use into the personal accounts he set up for you. If we split it up, then the company won't be able to get it."

I knew about the accounts. Dad wouldn't explain why he set up several accounts under my name, but he said it might be useful. That was almost six months ago. "Why would Frank Barlow try to take it? What about his company?"

Luke ran his hand through his hair. "Frank Barlow is the owner of CORE-TECH, the company your father did contracted work for. CORE-TECH paid your dad to come on sight once in a while. If you move the money now, you'll be able to keep it safe. I don't know if Frank has access to the company money, but I have to believe he will try. The last text I got from your dad suggested something bad was going on at CORE-TECH, and he was afraid Frank would somehow gain access to his company. Frank's brother was an employee of your dad. I would suggest you sell the stocks for your father's company, but that is up to you."

I narrowed my eyes, but he just got busy on the computer, accessing all the accounts. I had the feeling he wasn't telling me everything. Probably on strict orders from my father to protect me or something.

"Why do I need to sell the stocks?"

Luke ran a hand over his balding head. "Your father has it set up, so most of the work would be allocated to other subsidiaries in the event of his death. Frank doesn't know this and since his brother worked for your dad, I think he may try to liquidate the company to gain access to its funds. Illegally, I might add.

"I also want you to change the passwords to all the accounts and put the passwords in your father's safe."

"I don't know the combination." I was told I didn't need to worry about things like that.

Luke handed me a sealed envelope. "Your father gave me the code for safekeeping. Don't open it until I leave. I will step into the kitchen when it is time for you to change the passwords."

We spent the next hour transferring money and doing the necessary procedures to secure it. Two billion dollars? How had I not known my father was a billionaire?

When I opened my father's safe to put the passwords in it, I found an envelope with my name scribbled across the front in my father's handwriting. I set it on my father's desk, not wanting to deal with that today.

My mind was reeling when Luke left. I'd purposefully forced myself not to consider all Luke had told me while he was with me, but now that he was gone, I couldn't stop my brain from racing through it all. Dad had been hired by a company Luke seemed to think was corrupt...at least the owner was. Luke had found a picture of him on the internet. He appeared to be a regular businessman, the kind who made sure everyone knew how much money he had by wearing the most expensive shoes ever made. Mom would have been able to tell me the brand and even how much they usually sold for. I didn't care that much about how expensive people's clothes people were.

The encounter with the guy at the cemetery flashed through my mind. He knew me and Dad. Was he connected to Frank and trying to get to the company through me? The more I thought about it, the more I felt I didn't know my own father.

Chapter 2

Dear Alia,

We have had a vacancy come up in the Language Institute of Changhua and would like you to start your four-month teaching contract in January instead of waiting until April. Please let me know your decision within 48 hours so I can get tickets secured. I am excited to work with you here in Taiwan.

Sincerely,

Sara

Director of the Language Institute of Changhua

I stared at the email for a full minute before processing the words. I had applied when I'd thought Dad was being too protective. It was my one act of rebellion. Then I had told him about applying, and he had actually thought it was a good idea.

A boulder-sized lump settled in my stomach. Could I do this? I was still deep in my grief. I took a deep breath. Dad had agreed. He would never agree to anything he thought would bring me harm.

The walls closed in around me. It had been a week since Dad's funeral, and I'd only just managed to force myself to eat a little each day. I hadn't even gone outside. I had to get away from all of the memories.

Then I remembered the letter. I went to the study and plucked it from the desk. Maybe this would help me know what to do.

Dear Alia,

I fear I may be leaving you in a mess. I started doing work for CORE-TECH almost three years ago. About a year ago, I realized Frank Barlow was using his own company to cover up embezzling jewels. I approached the FBI. They gave me the option to get out, but they worried Frank would suspect I knew something. They asked me to stay to collect evidence. I helped gather a lot of evidence against Frank. I hope to get the information to help the FBI discover where he is sending the smuggled jewels. This should put Frank in jail. Yes, it is dangerous, but I feel it is my duty to do what is right, and this is right. I know it.

If I don't return, work with Luke to move your money into your accounts and get away for a while. I know you were planning on going to Taiwan in April, so maybe find somewhere else to go until then. Frank may try to find you at home. Promise me you will leave. Contact the FBI if you need to. The FBI will be watching you from afar, but reach out to Craig Phillips if you need anything.

Love, Dad.

Below his signature was Craig Phillips' number.

I quickly called Craig, figuring if Dad thought it important to include his number, I should tell him of my plans.

"This is Craig," a deep voice answered on the fourth ring.

"Hi," I said. " This is Alia Jepson. My father, Tray, left me a letter and told me to call you."

"Alia." Craig's rough voice softened. "How are you? I'm sorry about your dad."

I swallowed a sob. "Thank you. I was offered a four-month contract to teach English in Taiwan. My father left a note saying I should call, so I figured I should let you know my plans."

"You should be safe in Taiwan. We made sure you got offered a job sooner. We don't want you anywhere near Idaho Falls until we find Frank. We'll put someone in your apartment complex to keep an eye on things. Call me if anything happens or if you think someone might have followed you there."

My tongue stuck to the roof of my mouth. I pushed the fear down next to the grief and licked my lips. "Okay."

"I'll let you know when you're clear. Frank has disappeared, but with two billion dollars in the mix, he's sure to show."

My lungs expelled all the air in a whoosh. "You think he'll come after me?"

"Don't worry. We will have an agent in your apartment complex and another agent nearby."

"Okay." The FBI had made sure this email came. If that was the case, I was sure I should accept. I hung up with Craig, then hit reply and accepted the offer.

The next day, I got a response with the flight details. Two more weeks. The thought made my heart jump, but I was going to do this. I could be independent and take care of myself. Luckily, Dad had made sure I kept my passport current. At least it would give me something other than my grief and loneliness to focus on.

I needed someone to check on my house once in a while. Grace was the obvious choice since it wouldn't be hard for her. I made my way to Grace's house and knocked.

"Alia!" Grace said, then swung the door wider. "I have been so worried about you."

I forced a smile. "I'm doing all right." She wouldn't believe I was doing great since I hadn't been able to hide my puffy red eyes, no matter how much makeup I put on. "I actually have a job in Taiwan I am leaving for in two weeks."

"Taiwan?" Grace squealed. "Oh, if I was young again, I would beg to come with you."

"Can you check on the house once in a while? You know, make sure there's no problems?"

Some of the despondency drained out of me, leaving me feeling more exhausted. Grace's excitement was contagious. Maybe it would be fun. But it wasn't for fun. I was running to stay safe. I should tell Grace.

"I'm actually going to get away from a threat. I'm not sure what I can tell you, but as you keep an eye on my house, don't approach strangers. Call the cops. No one has permission to be at my house but you."

Grace looked confused, but thankfully she didn't question me.

I found the correct gate in Tokyo, then headed to the bathroom to freshen up. My make-up was smeared, and my hair pins were falling out. I pulled myself together, which would have made my parents proud, then found a seat near my gate. The handsome guy with the dark hair who sat next to me on the long flight from Seattle sat two seats away. He smiled at me, his blue eyes almost drawing me in. I twitched my lips in return. I had ignored him on the long flight, pretending I was sleeping, even though the air between us seemed tinged with static. The feeling scared me. I was glad he didn't try to talk to me.

He was reading a book. I fingered the sketchbook Grace had given me for Christmas. I tried to ignore the stranger next to me by sketching, but I couldn't get into it. Drawing and painting had once brought me joy, but now I was a shell of myself, and I couldn't even hold on to that important part of me. It had died with Dad and I wasn't sure I wanted it back.

The handsome stranger got up when my flight was called, and I stood behind him in line. He was a little taller than me, which was saying something since I was almost six feet. His dark hair curled over his forehead, and his skin was tanned. My eyes locked onto his biceps as he lifted his carry-on bag over his head. He glanced at me, and I immediately dropped my gaze. As luck would have it, I was sitting next to him again.

"Is Taiwan your final stop?" he asked as I settled my purse under my seat.

"Yeah."

"What are you doing in Taiwan?"

"Teaching English."

"Me too. The English Language Institute?"

My eyes widened.

"I was wondering when we were sitting next to each other for this flight, too," the stranger said. "Sara would have booked the flights together."

"But I just agreed to come two weeks ago."

"Me too." He stuck out his hand. "I'm Blake."

I shook his hand. "I'm Alia."

"So, are you excited to be going to a new country?"

My lips twitched into a small smile. I couldn't help myself. "How do you know I've never been there before?"

The boulder in my gut lightened a little, and I relaxed. The joke had been small, but it was the first bit of humor I'd found in weeks.

"Have you?" Blake asked.

I shook my head.

Blake leaned back in his seat. "Why did you take this job?"

"My dad encouraged me to take it." No need to tell him I applied before I told Dad about it. I was still surprised he had gone with the idea so willingly, but if the FBI had expedited the timeline, it made sense. "I wasn't supposed to come until April, but I guess they had a sudden opening."

"You needed encouragement?"

"No, that's not it. The job sounded exciting, but, well…" I stopped. My friends always made fun of me when I admitted my parents had such a strong hold on what I did. "Yes, I did want the job. I mean, I do want the job. But I graduated in Art Education, and this is teaching English and not art."

We fell into a companionable silence as the plane taxied onto the runway. Once I felt I could release my death grip on the armrest after take-off, exhaustion overtook me. I only woke when Blake elbowed me gently and indicated dinner was being served. Once my stomach was full, I succumbed to sleep again.

My eyes shot open when the wheels of the airplane hit the pavement and bounced. I grabbed at my armrest and ended up with a handful of Blake's arm. He patted my hand. His soft touch comforted me. I relaxed my grip and took my hand back. I avoided looking at Blake as I gathered my things, afraid he could see my embarrassment.

Anxiety tore through my throat. I wasn't sure I knew enough about the country. Dad had done his homework and explained what he found, but I still felt ill-prepared. I took a deep breath. Navigating my way to the driver Sara had promised would be easier with Blake. I'd stick close to him.

A nagging feeling in my gut tugged at the bottom of the pit that had formed after Dad's death. Everything at home was taken care of, yet something unsettled me. I told myself it was because I was moving to a foreign country where I didn't speak the language, but all that Luke had said hovered around me like fog. I had never met Frank Barlow, but if he did attempt to get the money, he would be disappointed. That thought scared me. I didn't know what he would do then. I hoped he would give it up and move on.

I stuck to Blake's side as we wound through travelers, looking for our driver.

Blake pointed at a guy with a sign that read "Alia Jeppson and Blake Hansen" written on it.

Blake started speaking rapidly in Chinese to him. He gestured to me, and I followed when they started walking, but I couldn't help but stare dumbly.

After stowing our luggage in the back of a van and climbing in, I finally found my voice.

"So, I'm guessing this isn't the first time you've been here," I said.

Blake shrugged. "I served a mission for the Church of Jesus Christ of Latter-Day Saints here."

The fact that he spoke the language was suddenly overshadowed by a need to connect in a different way. "You're a…could you…" My mouth couldn't seem to keep up with the thoughts stampeding through my mind. I let out a frustrated puff of air. "Do you already know of a ward for us to attend here?"

Having someone who spoke fluent Chinese would make going to church a lot easier.

"Yeah. We can go together if you want. You're a member, too?"

"Yes." Relief rushed through my body and lightened the anxiety rising in my chest. I wouldn't be alone here after all.

We fell silent, and I slipped into a fitful sleep. Blake nudged me awake what seemed like only minutes later.

"Alia. We're here."

The van pulled in front of a tall apartment building. A young man with curly dirty blonde hair stood next to a girl with a long brown ponytail, who was waving enthusiastically to us.

"Welcome to Taiwan!" The girl held her arms in a welcoming gesture as we climbed out of the van. "My name is Emma."

"I'm Anthony," the guy said, rushing to help the driver get our bags from the back.

Anthony turned his attention to me. "These yours?" he asked, holding up my bags.

"What gave me away?" I asked, knowing there weren't a lot of bags to choose from. But going with the joke broke up the pit in my stomach even more.

He winked. "Your name is on them."

"I haven't told you my name yet." I laughed and studied him more closely. His bright blue eyes reflected the light. He was my height, maybe a little shorter. And he was charming.

"Well, now would be a good time to supply that information, but you don't look like a Blake to me." His smile grew broader.

"I'm Alia."

"Let's show you to your apartment." Emma hooked her arm through mine and led me into the apartment building. "I get to be your roommate."

The spacious and neat lobby gave me hope we wouldn't get too many unwanted insect visitors.

"We're on the fifth floor." Anthony pushed the button in the elevator. "Blake and I are in apartment 503 and you and Emma are in 504."

"We'll all walk to work at 8 o'clock." Emma glanced at Anthony as if gauging to see if he agreed.

"Sounds good. We'll knock on your door when we are ready," Anthony said.

I looked at my watch. It was past midnight. My legs dragged like dead weight. The last time I had slept in a bed was a distant memory.

We turned left out of the elevator and stopped between two doors, one on either side of the hall. Emma opened the one on the left. Anthony set my suitcases just inside the door. Emma grinned, "Are you ready to explore your new home?" she asked.

"Yeah." I was relaxing around Emma. I could tell she would be a good roommate.

Emma stepped out of the way so I could walk into the apartment. A couch and chair faced a TV in the right front corner. The tiny kitchen had very little counter space and contrasted sharply with the large kitchen in my parents' home, which was perfect. I didn't need anything that reminded me of home right now.

Emma pointed to some house slippers next to the door. "It's customary to take your shoes off and wear house slippers. I bought you some. I hope they fit."

"Thanks." I quickly took off my shoes and donned the house slippers.

The slippers had rubber soles that gently tapped against the tiled floor as we made our way to the back of the room.

"Make sure you don't drink water out of the faucet, as it needs to be treated." She pointed to jugs of water. "We fill those for drinking water. There is a place to get treated water just down the street." She laughed. "It almost looks like a miniature gas pump."

I forced a smile, though my brain was spinning. How many other things would I have to remember?

Emma led me through an opening next to the kitchen. A hall led to two bedrooms with a bathroom sandwiched in between. Emma stopped at the first door.

"This is your room. The washer is at the back of the apartment, and we hang dry our clothes."

"Thanks," I said.

Emma patted my shoulder. "You look exhausted. Go to bed and try to sleep."

I stepped into the bathroom and was dismayed at the state of my hair.

Chapter 3

I closed the door to my new room and looked around. It was small and simple. I stepped out of my shoes onto the cold tiled floor in my room and gasped. Apparently, carpet wasn't the norm here. There was no window in my room, but that was fine.

I sat on the edge of my bed for a long time, despite my burning eyes. I needed sleep, but I felt numb. Blake was handsome and nice, and I was grateful for the help he had given me. Emma and Anthony were both friendly, but even with the people surrounding me, the loneliness that had become a familiar pit in my stomach just got stronger the farther I got from home. I had spent the long flight over the Pacific Ocean trying to convince myself it was silly to feel homesick. No one was at home, but right now it was a crushing weight against my chest and stomach making me feel nauseous. I rifled through my suitcases for the letter I had found in the safe deposit box. Reading my dad's words again made him feel close even if it was filled with warnings.

Tears coursed down my cheeks, and longing made my chest hurt. I wrapped my arms around my waist and struggled to silence my cries. I didn't need Emma coming in to see me like this. My mom regretted always telling me what to do. She told me so as she became sicker, but I missed it. I wanted my parents back, no matter what mistakes they thought they made in raising me.

I looked up what time it was in the United States and decided to call Craig. I wasn't going to fall asleep anytime soon, anyway.

"I made it to Taiwan," I said when he answered.

"I'm glad to hear it. I'll send you the picture of one of the agents watching you, just so you know him if you catch him following you. But make sure you don't interact with him and let on you know him."

"Thanks."

"His name is Daniel Collins."

My phone dinged.

"I just sent a picture of him. If you have problems, call me first, then I will let the agents know. Now, I believe it is the middle of the night over there. You better get some sleep."

I held back a "yeah, right" retort and ended the call. I studied the picture. Daniel had short light brown hair. He was clean-shaven. I guessed he was in his mid-thirties. How could I go to sleep knowing Frank Barlow might be coming after me?

Then everything clicked, and I slumped onto my bed. Why hadn't I made the connection before? If Frank was after me, that meant he probably had something to do with my father's death. It hadn't been an accident.

It wasn't until lunch the next day that I no longer felt like I was sleepwalking. My new boss probably sensed my exhaustion. Not the best first impression.

Little voices drifted up the stairs, and our lunch break ended. I was told to observe Anthony first, then Emma.

Anthony gathered his students at the bottom of the stairs. He introduced me and led the kids up the stairs singing "Mary Had A Little Lamb" with them.

We went into the kitchen first. Anthony demonstrated how to say different ingredients and talked through his actions, giving the kids a chance to repeat him.

"Lilly, what are we doing?" Anthony asked.

"Spreading jam," Lilly answered.

I walked beside Anthony as we made our way to the next room. "Is Lilly a Chinese name?"

Anthony shook his head. "They choose English names, and we address them by their English names in school."

"Why?" I asked.

"I don't know, really. Maybe it makes them feel like they are more immersed in their English learning."

I shrugged and stepped aside to let the children pass and brought up the rear. If the reason didn't matter, I wouldn't worry about it.

We switched groups, and I followed Emma to the gym, then up to a room that was filled with paper, markers, crayons, glue, and glitter. A smile slowly stretched my lips. I could handle this room. I considered myself an artist, and my parents had insisted I was really good, but admitting that felt like bragging. Emma helped the kids draw pictures of themselves.

I grabbed the dry-erase marker and stood at the whiteboard. "What should I draw?" I wondered out loud.

"Teacher Blake," one of the kids shouted.

"You barely met him," Emma said. "Why not a picture of me?"

"Draw teacher Blake," another kid chimed in.

Emma rolled her eyes in mock annoyance. The kids laughed.

I shrugged and drew a stick figure with shorts and a shirt and short hair. I almost added the loose curls that framed his face, but I didn't want to make a detailed sketch. First, because I didn't want to look like I was showing off. And second, because I didn't want to let on I had studied his chiseled face on the long flight here. I would blush for sure.

"Teacher Blake has big..." The student must not have known the word, so he flexed his muscles.

"Muscles?" I asked. I drew cartoonish-looking muscles on his arms and changed his position, so he was flexing.

A little girl called out, "Make him dance."

I grinned and erased his legs. I drew him standing on one leg with the other up to make him look like he was doing a pirouette. The kids howled with laughter.

A deep chuckle came from the door, and I whirled around. Blake's lips quirked up, and he wiggled his eyebrows. "I don't know if I've ever seen a better portrait."

He held my gaze for a moment. There was a look in his eyes I had never seen in anyone. Was it admiration? No, my dad had told me how great I was. My breath suspended in my lungs until I broke eye contact.

I fumbled with the eraser. Maybe if I erased the picture, I could pretend this awkward moment never happened. Now I was doubly glad I hadn't drawn a real-life sketch.

"What are you doing here?" Emma asked. "I thought you were observing Anthony."

Blake pushed off the doorframe. "Well, either Anthony let his class out early, or you kept yours late. When I heard my name, I couldn't help but stop and see what was happening."

Emma's eyes darted to the clock. "We still have five minutes." She focused on me. "Anthony has a bad habit of letting his class out early so he can joke around with them and the secretary while the kids wait for their rides."

I followed Emma down the stairs and ducked into the teacher's room while Emma said goodbye to the kids. I had a few New Taiwanese dollars—or kuài as Blake had called them—and wanted to get a snack at the 7-Eleven.

I slipped out the door. Halfway down the street, a cold shiver ran up my spine. I slowed my steps and peered into the shadows but couldn't see anything dangerous. I didn't even see a sign of Agent Collins. Maybe he was better at blending in than I thought possible for a white man in Taiwan, but my instincts were all I had. I turned on my heel and ran smack into Blake.

"Oh, sorry," I said, just as I caught sight of a white man near a building. Agent Collins wasn't shirking his duties even though I was out with people I knew. I was grateful for the added sense of security.

"Were you going to get something to eat?" Blake asked.

"Um, yeah."

"Changed your mind?" Blake's lips twitched.

"I don't know if I grabbed enough money." I wouldn't let Blake know I was scared, especially when I couldn't see any reason for the fissure of fear that had shot down my back. Most likely, it was paranoia.

"I'll cover you if you don't have enough. We don't have a lot of time before we have to be back." He lightly touched my elbow to steer me toward the 7-Eleven. Another shiver ran through me, but this time it felt good. Blake's fingers lightly caressed my arm as he dropped his hand.

"I am hungry," I admitted.

"And I need a break. It's a lot to take in."

I laughed. "Yeah. I can barely understand the kids sometimes, and they're supposedly speaking English."

"Don't worry, you'll get used to their accents soon enough. I'm probably not a good person to teach them since I speak Chinese. I found myself wanting to speak Chinese several times."

"They probably love that you speak their language." I reached up to touch his arm but stopped myself. I usually wasn't this open with someone I'd barely met, but Blake was different. I couldn't put my finger on why.

Chapter 4

Saturday morning, Emma knocked on my door before I had dragged myself out of bed.

"Come in," I called.

Emma opened the door a crack. "Hey! Anthony and I wanted to treat you and Blake to breakfast at food street. The boys will be here in a few minutes. Do you want to come?"

My first instinct was to say no, I wasn't ready. My mom would have died of embarrassment if I went out in public without being ready. Pleasing her memory was a way to keep her close. I closed my eyes, wracking my brain for a good excuse. When I met her eyes again, I noticed she was dressed in jeans and a t-shirt with little to no make-up on. I couldn't get away with no make-up, but maybe an easy hairdo would speed up my getting ready. Mom would probably turn in her grave, but I wasn't going to give up an opportunity to get to know my fellow teachers.

"Uh, sure."

"Great. I'll make sure they wait for you." She shut my door.

I scrambled out of bed, threw on some clothes, pulled my hair into a ponytail, and did all of my make-up. I smiled at my reflection. I couldn't see why my mom had insisted on fancy up-dos. The woman staring back at me was beautiful, even in a ponytail.

My hands shook as I reached for the doorknob, though. Knowing my mom wouldn't approve had guilt rising in me, threatening to suffocate me. The knowledge I had done my makeup helped me tamp it down. My friends probably wouldn't even notice. Emma wore a ponytail every day, and no one treated her any differently. With that final thought, I flung open the door and walked purposefully into my room to set my make-up bag on my desk.

I almost laughed at how defiant I felt. A sense of freedom bloomed inside of me. It was the first indication that coming to Taiwan would be a good thing, not just a way out.

Emma and Anthony led us a couple of blocks down the road.

When we turned the corner, I took a slight step back at the sheer number of mini restaurants and vendors on the short street. My eyes darted about, taking it all in; the brightly colored storefront awnings, the smells of food deep fat frying, and the people crowded around the open vendors. A white man with light brown hair caught my eye, and I quickly looked away. Agent Collins was never far away. For that, I was grateful. Some alcoves were closed, and fryer stands were pushed back into the recess of the building behind it. I took a deep breath through my nose and my stomach grumbled at the delicious smells wafting through the air.

"Welcome to food street," Emma said, weaving her arm around mine. "You will never be hungry as long as you can walk the block from our apartment to here."

She propelled me forward until we reached a place with a sign that read "Best Breakfast in Taiwan." Chinese characters covered the menu board. I glanced at Blake, then at Anthony and Emma. Did either of them know Chinese?

"Can we surprise you?" Anthony asked.

"Sure," I said.

Anthony stepped up to order. He spoke English, so I guessed the guy behind the Plexiglas understood enough to communicate. Anthony raised his voice and said something again.

Emma stifled a laugh. "We've never ordered from this guy before."

Blake stepped up behind Anthony. "Maybe I can help. What are you wanting to order?"

Anthony gave Blake a sidelong glance. "The things with the tortilla wrapped around cooked eggs with cheese and a yummy brown sauce inside."

Blake studied the menu for a minute, apparently figuring out what menu item matched what Anthony was describing. The man next to the grill waited somewhat impatiently, his eyes darting from Anthony to Blake. Blake cleared his throat and ordered for us in Chinese. The man's smile split his face, and he spoke animatedly to Blake for a minute before turning to the griddle to cook.

"Why didn't you tell me you could speak Chinese?" Anthony asked.

Blake shrugged. "It didn't come up."

We headed to Blake and Anthony's apartment to eat. I took another deep breath of the surrounding smells. A dog jumped out of the recess of another restaurant that probably would open later. I stumbled backward, tripping on someone's foot. Blake grabbed my arm to steady me. It was just a dog. Fear could not control me. I told myself there was no reason to be scared. I had no evidence anyone here was after me.

When we had finished eating—me using my unwieldy chopsticks like a two-pronged fork while everyone else nimbly ate using their chopsticks the proper way—Anthony turned to Emma, "What're we gonna show the newbies?"

"Hike Baguashan?" Emma suggested. "*And* the fitness trail."

"Get your walking shoes." Anthony winked at me. I cringed. Walking was fine, but Emma had said "hike." When I went hiking with friends, I was the one out of breath.

"Bawgwa...shawn," I repeated slowly.

Emma grabbed my hand and dragged me across the hall. "We'll meet you in the hall," she called to Anthony before the door shut.

"Are you ready for a little adventure?" Emma asked.

"It'll be better than sitting on the couch." I wasn't sure I believed my own words, but I didn't want Emma to know how nervous I was. I usually swam regularly, but I hadn't even done that for a couple months. Dealing with my dad's death had taken its toll.

"You ready to see the Big Buddha?" Anthony asked when Emma opened the door to find them waiting for us in the hall.

"Yeah." Now that I knew there was a big attraction at the end of the hike, maybe I could make it. Unpleasant flashbacks of waking up, lying on the grass next to the track in junior high with no idea of how I got there, flashed through my mind. The doctors determined it had to do with the impact of running, so I had turned to swimming and never had another problem. But I hadn't pushed myself that hard again, opting to swim at a slow, leisurely pace. I also had never competed again, certain the nerves had been to blame. The attention that episode brought me was agonizing, and I'd wished everyone would forget it ever happened.

"It's a famous attraction here in Changhua. It's probably two stories tall." Anthony's eyes held a hint of humor. I wondered what it would be like to always find the fun in life.

We set out with me at the rear, wondering if I could turn around and go back to my apartment without them noticing. The more I thought about it, the more I was sure I wouldn't make it to see the Big Buddha. I was going to make a fool of myself. My mom had demanded I remain poised at all times when in public. After passing out at the track, I wondered if I had disappointed her even though she'd never said anything about it. I never asked her, then a year later she had died. Anthony hung back to walk next to me. He stuffed his hands in his pockets as he kept pace with me, taking short steps. I had long legs, but I was terrified of appearing weak.

After a few blocks, we turned right. Soon we came to what Anthony called the University in Changhua. We wound our way around the campus buildings. The buildings loomed upon either side of us, gray and bleak even with the sun shining on them.

Anthony slowed to be next to me as I had lagged behind again with my thoughts. "We're going up a back way. The front entrance is on the other side of the hill, but it's closer for us to go this way."

I glanced at him to let him know I heard him but didn't know how to respond.

He winked. "I'll help you if you need it."

"I won't need help," I assured him. "I just haven't hiked in forever." I squared my back; I would prove to them and my father's memory—and maybe to myself—that I could do this hike. My throat pinched at the thought of Dad. I blinked rapidly to keep tears from forming. I missed him so much. I missed him, and I missed his guidance, even if I now thought it had stifled me. I would take Dad's overbearing company over being alone.

Blake looked back at me and Anthony. He paused for a moment to allow us to catch up.

We stopped at the bottom of a few stairs that led to a cement trail.

"Are you ready to experience hiking Taiwanese style?" Anthony asked.

I raised my eyebrows.

"Come on. It'll be fun." Anthony put his hand on my arm and nudged me forward. His touch was firm but reassuring. At least he would make sure I didn't fall off the mountain.

Emma started up the stairs, followed by Blake. Anthony motioned for me to go ahead of him. I steadied my breathing and took the four steps up to a level cement path.

After a few yards, the path forked. Emma turned right, crossing over a little red bridge that covered a gully in the hill, and suddenly, an endless line of stairs loomed in front of me. I stopped as I stared at Blake and Emma heading up.

Blake glanced back at me with concern in his eyes. "You look a little pale."

Curse my face for showing every emotion.

"I must still be feeling a little jetlagged." I figured that was a good enough excuse. Pushing my fears and worries away, I pasted a smile on my face. I would not let these guys think I needed to be carried or anything. Determination shot through my body, and I huffed up those stairs, refusing Anthony's arm for support.

I forced one foot in front of the other. After about ten steps, my thighs burned, and I had to push my body up by bracing a hand on each knee. This was nothing like swimming.

The steps were never-ending. Blake's gaze met mine, and he gave me a small nod. I concentrated on my feet to make sure I didn't trip, my heart skipping over itself.

Bushes and trees surrounded the stairs, so different from the sparse greenery I was used to seeing at home. I stopped that train of thought immediately before I started crying. Thinking of home would only end with me in a sobbing heap on the ground. I focused on the details around me, imagining paintings in my head. The trees had two or three trunks starting almost at the ground and had smooth bark. Spider webs gleamed in the sunlight that filtered through the leaves above me.

Soon my ragged breaths took my attention. I couldn't concentrate on anything other than climbing up the next step. My rapid breathing burned into my lungs. Would my heart explode before I got to the top? At least the pounding in my ears told me I was still alive.

Finally, we came to a flat area with no stairs. I searched the area for the Big Buddha but didn't see anything besides more trees. A gentle rise led up to the top of the hill. Luckily, there were no more stairs.

Anthony took my arm, leading me to a bench I hadn't seen.

I slumped onto it, too winded to even attempt to pretend I wasn't woefully out of shape. My heart beat so hard I thought it would jump out of my rib cage. I focused on my chest and watched it bounce slightly with every rapid heartbeat while expanding with my shallow breaths.

Chapter 5

I propped my palms against my knees, keeping myself from flapping forward. Anthony sat next to me with his hand resting on my back.

Blake crouched in front of me. "Are you okay?"

I nodded and blinked to keep tears from forming. My mom would be disappointed in my inability to remain poised. Blake patted my knee and rose.

"Do you think you can walk the rest of the way?" Anthony sounded sincere, so I met his eyes. The concern I saw there touched me. He got to his feet and extended his hand.

There was no way I was going to admit defeat now. I slowly put weight on my legs. Anthony held onto my hand while I dug deep for the strength to match my resolve. My knees wobbled, but the longer I stood, the stronger I felt. I took a few tentative steps and found that I could, indeed, still walk.

Blake's brow creased in concern as I wobbled forward. My father had taken me horseback riding when I was ten. He told the story so many times about how wobbly I was when I got off after riding for hours. At this point, I couldn't tell if I remembered the soreness or if my brain just supplied the constructed memory from hearing the story so many times. I laughed out loud.

"What?" Emma asked.

I shook my head. "I was just thinking about the one time I rode a horse. I'm pretty sure I walked like this after riding." My words cut off as a sharp tightness gripped my chest. At first, I worried I was having a heart attack, but when my eyes burned with unshed tears, I realized it was the memory of my father. Dad had walked next to me for a while to make sure I was sure of myself and safe before he got on a horse and rode next to me around the corral again and again, probably ready to catch me if I fell. Anthony moved his arm from my shoulder and cradled my forearm to steady me as my legs trembled.

"Are you ready to keep going?" Blake asked.

I met his eyes. "Yeah, I am. Where is this Big Buddha you guys were talking about?"

"Behind those buildings." Emma pointed to two towers that rose to the sky. The hexagon roofs sloping slightly, then shooting straight out from the building reminded me of pictures from my history book.

After we had gone about a hundred yards, my legs stopped feeling shaky and fell into the familiar groove of walking.

We made our way around the towers. Then I saw the back of the Big Buddha. A large building stood right behind it, and smaller, long buildings lined either side of the main courtyard where the big Buddha sat. Excitement tickled my insides. The sights were all so new, and I wanted to take them all in.

Anthony steered me toward a building by the statue, and Blake and Emma followed. "We'll show you the Buddhist Temple before we see inside the statue." Anthony led me upstairs next to a small rock statue of an elephant and entered a red building. Two large staircases were divided by a large slab of stone with dragons carved into it, making the dragons' heads appear to be coming out of the stone. Inside, a large room with a cavernous ceiling made the inside seem huge and filled with beautiful statues that probably depicted the important things of Buddhism. Candles flickered around statues of lions and other animals as well as tall, beautiful women draped in robes. In front of the statues was a small table with an ornate tablecloth. A few sticks of incense burned in stands on the table.

"This is beautiful." The reverence in the building was a stark contrast to the bustling city that surrounded the large hill where the Buddha sat.

"Come on." Anthony pulled on my arm. "Let's go see the main attraction."

I took a deep breath, hoping to absorb the peace I felt here.

Inside, the Big Buddha was muggy and stifling and after only a few minutes inside, I was ready for some fresh air. I escaped the Buddha into the open air outside, though it was still warm and muggy—not the weather I was used to for New Year's Eve.

We went to the front of the Big Buddha. I took in the huge statue. The Big Buddha's hands were folded in front of him on his crossed legs. He had on a sort of robe which hung down, exposing part of his chest. His earlobes were very large. I wished I knew if that was how Buddha really looked. The statue's face made him appear to be in deep meditation.

I turned to say something to Emma, but to my dismay, I found myself staring into the eyes of a kindly Taiwanese gentleman. I searched frantically about and saw them heading toward the Buddhist Temple.

A hand on my elbow made me jump. It was Blake.

"Sorry, I didn't mean to startle you." He smiled.

I sighed, though I was embarrassed he might have seen me freaking out. Getting lost in a foreign country would not be good. The intense fear of getting lost had been a companion of mine for a long time. Ever since my parents lost track of me at the fair when I was ten. Strangers surrounded me, and I didn't want to show them my fear, so I ran and hid in a tent. I hadn't realized the loudspeaker from the stands was calling me there to find my parents for a while.

After that, I had been content to stay by my parents' side. Now that I thought about it, it was why having them both gone scared me so much. I blamed myself. Weren't you supposed to get the urge to spread your wings and fly from the nest? It had never happened for me, and my parents certainly hadn't forced the issue.

Halfway to the staircase that would take us off the mountain, Anthony stopped. "Oh! You guys have to try the 'fitness trail'." Anthony put up air quotes and grinned.

"What's the fitness trail?" I asked the same time Blake rolled his eyes. I had feeling he knew what they were talking about and what they had planned.

"Why don't we do it another time? Alia didn't fare so well on the hike up here."

"We'll show you and you can decide." Anthony led us a little off the sidewalk through some bushes and trees. There was a path with rocks cemented in, but they weren't level; most were sticking out anywhere from half an inch to a quarter of an inch.

Emma spoke up. "I walked the entire fitness trail—barefoot. This is supposed to be the end, but it's the hardest part, so if you can get past this, then you're well on your way to being able to finish. Anthony only made it one length." She elbowed Anthony lightly.

Anthony laughed at Emma's teasing. "I just didn't think it was worth torturing my feet to be able to say I did it."

I caught Blake's eye, hoping he would give some sort of explanation.

"We really can come back and do it later if you really want to. You don't have to do it today."

My insides warmed at his words.

"I'll do it with you then," he went on, "though Taiwanese people don't walk the trail, they use it as a way to massage their feet."

Emma gaped. "What? I guess the teachers before us used it as a rite of passage."

I stood at the edge of the path, wondering what I should do. According to Anthony, it hurt. Blake said I could bow out, but how would that look to Anthony and Emma? It would just prove I was weak.

"I can join that rite of passage." I straightened my spine, determined to go through it with as much grace as possible.

"I suppose you want us to take off our shoes?" Blake asked.

"Well, yeah," Anthony said sarcastically. "I would have walked the whole thing if I could keep my shoes on."

I caught Blake's eye.

"You don't have to do this," he mouthed.

Yes, I did. Especially if he didn't think I had it in me. I slipped off my shoes, held them in my hand, and waited to follow Blake onto the path. I'm sure if my feet knew the torture, I was going to put them through, they would have sent messages to my brain to keep me from ever taking a step on that rocky path. As it was, they didn't know, so we started walking. The big rocks cut dully into my feet sending pulses of pain to my brain. After a few steps, I avoided the biggest ones as much as possible, though stepping on the little rocks felt like stepping on needles.

We made it to a smooth reprieve in the path. We shuffled to the next part where the rocks loomed ahead: veritable boulders to climb over, even though they were sticking less than an inch out of the cement. Before we stepped on the next part of the rocky path, Blake raised an eyebrow in question. Did I want to continue? Well, I didn't want to, but I started this day determined to show how *not* weak I was, and I wouldn't back down now.

Each step was painfully slow. I attempted to walk faster, but speed increased the intensity of pinpricks of pain shooting through my foot and up my legs. We got to the next flat spot in the path and rested for a second before continuing. The rocks in the next section were more uniform.

After an eternity, Anthony announced, "Okay, this is the final stretch."

Anthony winked. I smiled, encouraged, but also slightly embarrassed at his attention.

I glanced at Blake. He met my gaze and held up his hand. I stared at it a moment—my pride warring with my necessity—before taking it. I could use all the support I could get. Blake squeezed my fingers and warmth ran up my arms and into my chest. Blake moved onto the rocks. We started the final stretch of our self-inflicted painful journey. I couldn't believe I was purposefully doing something to hurt myself. The weird thing was, pride expanded my chest, and it felt good, contrasting sharply with the needle-like sensation in my feet.

My steps were jerky, and I swayed side-to-side, trying to relieve pressure from my feet as much as possible. The rocks were all small now but lacked any reprieve between them.

My toes came away from the ground of their own accord, retreating from the rocks. My toes reaching to the sky only made the pain in the middle of my foot even more unbearable. Another squeeze from Blake brought my focus to the end of the path. We were almost there. The swelling in my chest expanded even more.

"I can't believe I did that," I gasped, stepping off the end of the path. Blake squeezed my hand. "I can't believe I did that!" I repeated, squealing.

Blake laughed. "You were awesome."

Before I could talk myself out of it, I extricated my hand from Blake's and flung my arms around him. I was so proud of myself. I had done two hard things in one day and I had made the decision to do them. Nobody had told me whether or not I should. It had been my choice. I drew away from Blake and grinned.

My phone vibrated in my pocket, so I turned away to see who it was. Luke had texted. I waved at the others. "You go ahead and get started. I just have to answer this text."

They all cocked their heads.

I waved them away. "I'll catch up if you go slow."

They each started walking. Blake stopped a few paces away. When I was sure they wouldn't read over my shoulder, I opened the text.

Luke: Alia. Are you well? Grace, your neighbor, called me. She said a guy has come by several times trying to get into your house. He claimed he was from the gas company, then the plumbing, then the electric company. Grace wanted me to check on you. She said the guy tried to disguise himself, but she could tell it was the same guy.

Me: I'll call Grace later. Do I need to do anything?

Luke: The police might question you, but Grace never got the guy's name so we can't ID him. And he managed to hide his face from the security cameras. I just wanted to let you know that someone is either looking for you or for a way to get the money.

Me: Will the money stay safe?

I didn't really care about the money, but if Frank could get to the money, what else would he be able to take from me?

Luke: Yes. Stay vigilant, though. If they get it without getting caught like we planned, they will try to find you.

A shiver of fear coursed through me. Yes, Luke had planted some red herrings for Frank to follow, hoping he would fall for it and get caught. I guess that hadn't happened yet.

Me: Thanks.

I wasn't sure if I should say anything about the FBI agent Dad had connected me with. They would keep me safe. Frank wouldn't be able to track me here that easily, would he? How would he know I left the country?

Blake was still waiting for me. Emma and Anthony were out of sight. Shoving my phone in my pocket, I hurried to him.

"Is something wrong?"

I shook my head. "It's nothing. Just something from home I need to be aware of."

Blake's skeptical look told me I hadn't convinced him, but I looped my arm around his and pulled him forward.

Chapter 6

I went directly to my bedroom when we returned. My eyes burned. Was the person who showed up at my house after the money? Did they really think I would hide everything in my home? Luke had instructed me to write false passwords and leave them in the study, but that was to slow them down so police could get there if needed. But so far, the person hadn't tried to break in, they had asked Grace to let them in. They had to have known about the silent alarms. Would they try to find me now that they hadn't made it in the house? My chest tightened. I gasped as a sob escaped, then lay on my bed, curled my legs to my chest, and let myself cry, being careful to keep quiet. The pain was mostly because I wished things were different. I wished I was here with the ability to call or text my dad whenever I needed him.

Closing my eyes, I focused on happy memories.

"Alia!" Emma called.

I jerked awake.

"In here," I yelled back.

Emma opened the door, took one look at me, then rushed to me. "Alia? What's wrong?"

I let the silence hang between us, deciding what to tell her. It would be nice for someone to know what I was going through.

"My dad died almost a month ago," I whispered. "I'm just missing him."

Emma's sympathy was immediate. "I'm so sorry. That must be so hard."

"Thanks."

"Anthony and I were thinking about going to a firework show at the University for New Year's Eve. Do you want to come with?"

"Yeah. I'd like the distraction."

Before Emma could respond, someone knocked on the door.

"That must be them."

I headed to the bathroom. "I'll be out in a minute." No need to let everyone know I had been crying.

When the four of us got to the field at the University, it was so crowded we stood on the side of the track. A stage was set up at one end, a karaoke machine on top.

Emma immediately bounced with the music. "Are you going to come sing with me?"

"Me?" I swiveled my head from left to right to be sure she wasn't talking to someone else. She was staring at me. "I'm not a good singer."

"Who cares? I've never heard a rule that says you have to be a good singer to sing karaoke."

True, but I'd never been one to put myself in the spotlight. What if someone had followed me here but hadn't found me? I would be showcasing myself to them. No. I was not going to live in fear. And the odds that someone could have shown up at my house a day ago then come all the way here and found me at a New Year's Eve fireworks show was so low, it was laughable.

"Come on. Come sing with me," Emma urged.

I allowed her to pull me on stage, willing myself to relax. Singing karaoke wouldn't kill me.

Luckily, they had some English songs we could sing. Emma chose the classic *YMCA*.

After the first verse, the shouting and cheering loosened me up, and I swung my hips and did the actions with gusto.

I searched the audience to find Anthony and Blake. They stood near the stage singing along with us. My parents would be so proud of me. My throat constricted and I stopped singing.

Stumbling off the stage, I staggered through the crowd, looking for some place I could collect my emotions in privacy.

I found a little bench dimly lit by the lights at the stadium. I fell into it and let out dry sobs. No tears formed, but my breaths came in gasps, and I couldn't breathe.

"Alia?"

I started and turned to see Emma coming to join me.

"Are you okay?"

I nodded, not trusting my voice.

Emma put her hand on my shoulder. "I'm sorry. Wrong question. I can see you're not okay. What's wrong? I'm sorry if I pushed you too hard to sing with me. I thought we were having fun, but—"

"No," I interrupted. "It wasn't that. I..." I broke off. She already knew about my dad's death.

Emma didn't push me to continue. Silence enveloped us. My throat constricted in an effort to keep from crying.

I took a deep breath. Emma continued to study me as I struggled with my emotions. My breath caught slightly when I looked at her, distracted for a moment. The light from the stadium shining behind her silhouetted her head, making her glow.

She would make a great model for a drawing. I could already see the picture in my mind. It would be titled "BEAUTIFUL, INSIDE AND OUT."

"So...?" Emma prompted.

I shook my head to get rid of my musing, no matter how welcome of a reprieve it was. Emma gestured for me to continue.

"I just thought of how proud my mom and dad would have been for putting myself in the spotlight. It reminded me of how they encouraged me. My dad's death has just made me remember the pain of losing my mom as well." I took a deep breath and blew it out hard. The tears I had been fighting against finally burst from my eyes and slid down my cheek. I wiped them away and struggled to regain control. The anguish crushed my chest, but I refused to let more tears fall.

"Alia?"

I jumped and saw Blake standing a few feet behind us. I searched the area for Anthony but couldn't see him.

Blake made his way around to the front of the bench and sat next to me. He put a hand gently over mine, gripping the front of the bench.

"It's okay to miss them. And to grieve."

I thought of my father's funeral. I had grieved, or thought I had, but then that guy had shown up. Anger flared inside of me as I remembered his words. I knew they weren't true. Since he had followed his statement about keeping my father home with questions about the money, it made sense he would say something to get my guard down a little, hoping I would slip some information.

"He had been trying to manipulate me," I mumbled.

"What?" Blake asked. "Who was trying to manipulate you?"

I looked at him, then at Emma. "A guy came to me after the graveside service of my father and told me I could have kept him alive. But he asked questions about the company. I think he was trying to catch me off guard so I would give him information."

"Why would someone want to know about your father's company?" Emma asked. "Did he have shares in it or something?"

"I guess." I didn't really want to go into how much money my dad had.

Blake squeezed my hand, let go, and stood up.

"Do you want to go back home, or do you want to stay for the fireworks?" Blake asked.

"I want to stay for the fireworks."

Blake offered me his hand.

I hesitated a moment. My gaze moved from his hand to meet his eyes.

He smiled slightly, the shadows on his face making him mysterious, but inviting. I took his hand, and he led me through the crowd to where Anthony was watching the singers. Blake didn't drop my hand until we stopped, and the loss of contact made me feel vulnerable.

The fireworks lit the night sky and then boomed. I jumped as the first one went off. I lost my balance and Blake caught my arm and steadied me. His touch brought me comfort and helped me forget the memories of that day in the cemetery.

Chapter 7

The next morning, I walked next to Blake as he led the way to church. I had invited Emma, but she had politely declined. The warmth from Blake's touch was something new, and I didn't know what to make of it.

"Is everything okay?" Blake said after a long silence.

"Umm, yeah." I missed my parents and was still grieving their loss, but I was managing.

"Does it have to do with last night?"

I shrugged.

Another long pause. "I'm sorry about your dad." Blake's voice was soft, and I had an inexplicable urge to unload everything on him.

I waited until the urge passed, then simply smiled. "Thanks."

"Do you want to tell me about him? What about your mom?"

"My mom died when I was fourteen. My dad owned his own accounting firm. He worked with businesses all over the world, so he was gone a lot, but always made time for me. He would tell me I was his whole world. My mom was strict about looking my best all the time, but she was very kind and compassionate. Dad made sure we kept her memory alive by looking at pictures and reliving memories. She made me feel like I was the most important person on the planet."

"It sounds like they loved you."

"They did. They had to work hard to even have me, so they might have overcompensated by being overprotective and involved in my life. Being in a big crowd probably made me more emotional last night. I've never loved being in crowds for long."

"That's something we have in common. I prefer time alone over time at a party or event."

"I should have guessed that. You are the complete opposite of Anthony. I don't think Anthony stopped talking to me the whole time I was wobbling down the stairs yesterday." I giggled at the memory then pushed Blake's arm playfully. "I wouldn't have walked like a goose if you hadn't been okay with walking that fitness trail. I blame you."

He lifted his eyebrows. "Hey, I tried to give you an out. You were the one who insisted we do it. But…admit it. You were proud of yourself."

I focused on the sidewalk. "I haven't really done anything I didn't want to do, and my parents never forced me to push myself. I was proud for finishing something that felt so impossible."

Blake nudged me with his elbow. "You should be." He grabbed my elbow and steered me to a tan, three-story building. "This is it. Do you want me to translate for you?"

"That would be great."

As soon as church started, peace enveloped me, and I breathed it in deeply. As I sat through the sacrament portion of the meeting, I felt my parents' presence. Tears ran silently down my cheeks, and Blake put his arm around me and gave my shoulders a squeeze. Then he kept his arm there—a constant reminder I wasn't as alone.

After church, the ward members congregated in the kitchen. They had a big pot full of yellow chicken curry. One of the ladies passed out some bowls, and we dished up.

"This is delicious," I said after taking a bite.

"It is one of my favorites." Blake held the bowl close to his face, using the chopsticks like a seasoned pro.

"Maybe you could make sure I try all the best foods while I'm here."

"Mission accepted." Blake grinned, but then his eyes grew serious. He shook his head and returned his attention to his bowl.

I started my first session with my evening level 1 class by asking the students to tell me what they liked to do. After each student said something—mostly something about video games and liking to speak Chinese—I moved on with the lesson. One girl's hand went up in the air. My face burned a little when I couldn't remember her name. "I'm sorry. What was your name again?"

"Elaine," she said quietly, her long black hair falling in front of her face as she ducked her head.

"Elaine, thanks for reminding me. What did you need?"

"Teacher? You not tell us what you like."

"Oh. Umm...I like to draw, and..." I paused. I couldn't think of anything else. "And paint."

"You are artist?" another student asked.

"I guess." I wanted to move on with the lesson. I hadn't been able to immerse myself in my art since my dad's death and just the thought of drawing made my throat constrict, so I had to clear it several times.

"You are probably good artist," Elaine said. "You very pretty. I think you probably make pretty pictures."

Tears stung the back of my eyes, but I blinked them away. Almost immediately, my heart burst wide open for these children. They saw something good in me without even knowing me. I decided I would give my all to them during my time here.

When I got to the teacher's lounge after the classes left for the evening, I noticed a text from Luke.

Luke: Grace caught a guy getting ready to wash your windows and called the cops, but he insisted you paid him. Since they didn't have anything solid, and he wasn't Frank, they had to let him go.

Me: Who was it?

Luke: They won't tell me. Maybe you can get a name from them.

Me: I'll call when I get home. What time is it there?

Luke: Five in the morning.

Me: Someone was trying to wash my windows before business hours?

Luke: That was what tipped Grace off. Luckily, she is a light sleeper, and she saw the headlights pull up. She called the police immediately, then she called me.

Me: Thanks.

As soon as I got home, I rushed to my room and shut the door. I slipped my phone out of my pocket and dialed Craig Phillips's number, hoping he would answer even if it was early.

"Hello?" came the gruff voice.

"Mr. Phillips. This is Alia Jepson. Sorry to call you so early."

Craig cleared his throat. "I was awake anyway."

"I was told someone claimed I paid them to wash windows, but they were there an hour ago."

"Yeah. My guys watched him, waiting for an opening to catch him by surprise. Your neighbor called the cops before the guy even started washing windows."

"Who was it?"

"He claimed his name was Riley Sanders. Since the police showed, and we didn't have proof that this incident was part of our jurisdiction we had to let them do what they wanted."

"Do you have any idea what they were after or if they knew I was gone?"

"I don't know." Craig's voice was tight. "I'm sure they are trying to figure out a way to get that money. You didn't leave anything that would give them any clues, did you?"

"Luke had me plant false passwords and accounts in the office in case they tried to break in to give the police time to catch them, but they must know about the silent alarms. I've been wondering if I should tell you about a guy who showed up at my father's grave after everyone left." I quickly told him what the guy had said.

"Yes, if your dad had stayed home, he might be alive, but that has nothing to do with you. He didn't listen to me most of the time."

I smiled at that. I believed it. My dad had been very stubborn.

"You haven't seen this man there, have you?" Craig asked.

"No."

"I'll let my guys in Taiwan know."

"Thanks. Any lead on Frank?"

"No," Craig grumbled. "I can't believe he has eluded us so completely."

The next day, my stomach was tied in knots, making eating breakfast impossible. Frank—if that was who was behind the people going to my house—would realize soon he wouldn't be able to get to my money that way. Then his attention would turn to finding me. The positive point this morning was I would be teaching with Blake. It was easy to be myself around him, and I desperately wanted to feel like myself.

"Hey, Alia," Blake said as I entered the teachers' lounge.

"Hey," I replied, glad he couldn't see my heart tripping over itself.

He leaned against the wall with his hands in his pockets. His dark hair curled at the end, bringing my attention to his blue eyes. "What do you want to teach?"

I shrugged and searched for a spot to stare at besides his face. I couldn't help blurting out, "Art."

"You must really like art. Didn't you teach it on your rotation with Anthony?"

"Yeah." Teaching art was igniting my desire to open my own art studio—a dream I had never voiced aloud since I knew my parents would tell me it was impractical. That was why I went into art education.

Blake shifted slightly, bringing my attention to his well-toned arms. I shifted my gaze to a spot behind him, fighting the heat creeping through my neck.

"Do you have any other preferences?" he asked.

"Not gym." I forced a laugh. "I mean, you saw me try to climb up to the Big Buddha."

He chuckled. "I can do gym," he said. "Do you mind if I do kitchen?"

I forced myself to meet his gaze again. He lowered his eyes momentarily before bringing his attention to my face.

"Yeah," I answered. "I can teach games and art."

We ate lunch with Anthony and Emma, then headed down to start our rotations. We split the kids into two groups and started our classes.

Blake stood in the hallway when it was time to switch. Someone touched my elbow. Blake's hand rested on my forearm. I forced myself to make eye contact, though I felt a little embarrassed at his attention. He gave my arm a squeeze. I smiled in spite of myself.

"Teacher?" One of the kids' voices brought me out of my thoughts.

I shook my head slightly. "How about we play memory today?"

Chapter 8

Two weeks later, Emma found me in my bedroom. "I have a home visit tomorrow. What about you?"

I shook my head.

"I think Blake and Anthony also have home visits. What are you going to do?"

I showed her the guidebook I was flipping through. "I think I might see a place called Fire Water Cave. It's near a city called Guanziling. I just have to get a train ticket to Chaiyi, then find a bus to Guanziling." I had been thumbing through the book for a week, searching for both the courage to go somewhere and a place that caught my eye. I wanted to go somewhere alone. It frightened me, but I wanted to be independent. I hadn't gone anywhere on my own besides the grocery store and classes.

You're going alone?" she asked.

"Yeah." When I saw the concern in her eyes, I went on. "I'll be fine. It'll be good for me, right?" It was time I made my own decisions, even if it scared me. I would beat my fear and prove to myself and my father's memory I was capable of taking care of myself. I was grateful Craig hadn't called to tell me Frank had got on a plane here. I couldn't go out alone if I knew he was in the country. Agent Collins would be nearby, anyway.

I had to ask Blake about tickets, but I figured I'd run to food street to grab some dinner first. The elevator doors opened with a ding.

"Alia!"

I jumped and put my hand on my chest. It was Anthony.

Anthony smiled. "Sorry, I startled you. Are you going to get dinner?"

I nodded, my heart still racing at his sudden appearance.

"Mind if I join you?"

"Not at all."

We stepped into the elevator. It wasn't until we were walking down the darkened street that Anthony broke the silence.

"I heard Emma has a home visit tomorrow, but you don't. What are you going to do?"

"Sightsee."

"Sounds fun." He was quiet for a moment. "I don't feel like we know each other very well. Where are you from?"

"Idaho Falls, Idaho."

Anthony cocked his head at me. "Your last name is Jepson?"

"Yes."

"You don't happen to be related to Tray Jepson, do you? He was in Forbes magazine as one of the most successful start-up companies for last year."

That was news to me. "He's my dad."

"Holy smokes! I need to meet him. I have a bunch of business ventures I want to try."

I hadn't told Anthony about his death. I guessed Emma and Blake hadn't mentioned it, either. "He died at the end of November."

Anthony slid his arm around me. "I'm sorry, Alia. I can't believe I didn't hear about it. I'm sure it was all over the news."

Or the FBI wanted to keep it quiet. And I hadn't bothered putting an obituary in the newspaper. It was all too overwhelming. Maybe Grace had. I would have to check.

"Sorry to be a downer." Anthony gave my shoulder a squeeze and let his arm drop. "So, what happens with your father's company?"

I shrugged. "I'm not sure. He had it all squared away with his lawyer, but I don't know the particulars."

"Sorry to bring up bad memories. When did you decide to come to Taiwan?" he asked, clearly wanting to change the subject.

"A few months ago. I wasn't supposed to come until April, but I got an email that said they had an earlier opening, so I took it."

"You *and* Blake, huh? I thought the teachers you replaced were staying an extra four months, but out of the blue, they both went home early."

"How long have you been here?" I asked.

"Since the beginning of September. Emma and I came at the same time."

"Why did you decide to teach if you are interested in starting your own business?"

"The thing about starting your own business is that it often takes money. Instead of getting a loan, I figured I'd work and Taiwan seemed fun." He scrunched his nose. "Though… teaching little kids isn't my favorite thing. Don't tell them I said that. I like hanging out with them."

"How long are you going to stay?"

He lifted one shoulder. "I'm not sure. How about you?"

"I'll go home in April."

We got to a vendor on food street and ordered our food.

"Do you mind if I get a selfie with you?" Anthony asked.

"I guess." I held my food and smiled as he snapped a picture of us.

"Thanks." We were quiet as we ate our food and headed back to the apartment. After a few moments of silence, Anthony broke it again. "The kids seem to love you. How do you do it?"

I shrugged, though I was pleased that he had heard that. "I didn't know they loved me. I just do my best to connect with them."

He studied me, his eyes serious. "You are very relatable. Unlike me."

"You're a great friend," I countered.

His eyes twinkled. "Just friends?"

I laughed. "Yes. Just friends."

He sighed dramatically. "I was afraid of that, but I've seen how you look at Blake."

Heat crept up my neck. "I didn't think I was that obvious." Did Blake notice? Was he making sure I knew we were just friends as well? I put my free hand on my face, willing it to cool.

Anthony nudged me. "Hey, you don't need to be embarrassed."

We had reached the apartment complex doors.

"I think I'm going to eat out here," Anthony said. "It's a nice night. Do you want to join me?"

"No thanks. I need to ask Blake how to get train tickets."

Anthony winked. "I'll take my time."

I ducked my head, and Anthony's laughter rang through the night air.

I hurried to Blake's apartment with my half-eaten dinner. Eating dumplings and walking slowed me down. I usually ate on food street, but Anthony had headed back so I had followed. Now they were cold. Gross. I dumped the rest of my dinner in a garbage can near the elevator before knocking on the door.

Blake opened the door almost immediately. "Hey Alia."

"Hi." My face heated again thinking of my conversation with Anthony. I forced myself to be casual.

Blake motioned to the couch, and I sat down. He settled next to me, and I immediately leaned into him, then caught myself. I didn't need to set myself up for heartbreak before I knew how Blake felt.

"What can I do for you?"

"Could you show me how to see the train schedules, so I can figure out what time to leave in the morning?"

"Where're you going?"

"Chaiyi."

"Alone?"

I nodded. "It will be fine. I need to do this." I couldn't tell him I would have an FBI agent following me.

Blake stood. "Sounds fun. Let me get my computer."

A moment later, he returned and set his laptop on my lap.

"Type in 'Taiwan train schedule'," he instructed. "Click on the title that is all in Chinese."

I followed his instructions. "Hopefully, I remember all this if I have to plan another trip."

"You can always ask me to refresh your memory," he said.

My cheeks warmed again. I focused on the computer so he wouldn't notice how much he affected me. "Okay...Now what?"

He walked me through finding when trains stopped in Chaiyi that left Changhua. Blake handed me a small piece of paper with the time the train departed, along with a few other Chinese characters.

"Go to the ticket counter and give them this. I wrote that you want to take the local train to Chaiyi at this time. Get there plenty early." He handed me the piece of paper. "I could go in and get your ticket for you..."

"No. I need to do this."

Blake held my gaze for a moment. "I'm proud of you."

I stared for a second longer. He was proud of me?

"It takes a lot of guts to travel by yourself in a country where you don't speak the language."

"Yeah... I came to Taiwan to be brave."

"Well, let me get your number in case you run into trouble and need a translator."

Warmth and relief spread through my body. Having Blake's number would help ease my anxiety. I handed him my phone, and he texted himself so he would have my number.

"Thanks," I whispered and left.

I returned to my apartment and called Craig to tell him of my plans.

The next morning, after a quick breakfast, I rode to the train station and had to take several deep breaths to get up the courage to walk in.

I tried to appear confident as I approached the ticket counter where a Taiwanese lady with short, bobbed hair greeted me.

Digging Blake's note from my pocket, I gave it to her. She handed me a ticket and pointed to the amount I owed. I dug the money out of my purse and thanked her in Chinese.

The trains heading south left from platform one, so I put my ticket through the machine to let me in and found a seat near the entrance, taking deep breaths. My heart felt fluttery, and my hands were sweaty.

As I got closer to Chaiyi, my anxiety grew. Doubts about whether I would get off at the right station or be able to find the bus that would take me to Guanziling bombarded me as quickly as I could fight them. I scanned the train car and saw Agent Collins sitting in a seat near the back of the car. I didn't acknowledge that I knew him, but relief spread through me. Having an agent follow me was a good baby step to truly traveling by myself. The sign at the head of the train car flashed letters saying Chaiyi was the next stop, so I stood and held onto the handles hanging from the ceiling. I stepped onto the platform and followed the signs to the exit. It wasn't until after I had put the ticket into the slot and exited the station that I remembered I would have to get a return ticket.

Chapter 9

Thinking I would be stuck in Chaiyi forever, adrenaline shot through my veins. It was followed shortly by anger at Blake for not mentioning it, which was quickly overridden by guilt for even blaming him. I was the one who had insisted I could take care of myself. I set my shoulders and told myself I would be fine. I repeated "I can handle this" over and over in my head. After a minute, I started feeling…maybe I could. There was a bus station right next to the train station, so I went there, hoping someone could point me in the right direction.

A man met me outside the bus station and asked, "Alishan?"

I shook my head. "Guanziling," I said, probably butchering the pronunciation

He started speaking Chinese, but he pointed to the road and gestured to the right facing road in front of the train station. I thanked him and headed that way. When I got to the corner, I studied the map in my guidebook. Soon I was at the bus station. My chest expanded in much the same way it had when I finished walking the fitness trail. I found the bus station! I felt like dancing.

The sign listing locations and when buses left was long. I couldn't make heads or tails with the characters and numbers.

"Where you going?"

I jumped and turned to see a man in a bus uniform grinning at me. Opening my guidebook, I pointed to the word *Guanziling*.

The man nodded. "Bus leaves at nine o'clock."

I glanced at the clock on the wall. That meant I only had five minutes to wait. I paid for the fare, and he gestured to follow him, and he led me to another man. "This, driver of bus."

The man told the bus driver where I was headed. At least I heard the word Guanziling mentioned. The bus driver beckoned for me to follow him onto the bus. He took my ticket and tore the corner off. I sat right behind the driver, confident he would make sure I got to the correct place.

About twenty minutes into the bus ride, I saw a sign for Guanziling. I rose from my seat, but the bus driver caught my eye in his mirror and shook his head. *Relax, Alia. He knows where you want to go. He'll make sure you get off at the right time.* It was hard trusting a man who didn't speak the same language as I did. I looked around for Agent Collins, but he wasn't on the bus. He was probably somewhere close, following along in a rented car. No one besides Grace, Luke, and the FBI knew I was here, anyway. There was no reason to be nervous. My breathing came in shallow gasps, but I forced my breathing to slow. This was the moment for me to show I could handle the independence I had insisted I needed. If I did get lost, I could call Blake.

The man stopped to pick up more passengers, and Agent Collins got on. The way he could get around amazed me. I was sure he found a different stop to be sure we weren't connected.

After climbing steep roads for a while, the bus turned into a parking lot in a small town. The driver gestured this was my stop. He stopped me before I got off and showed me a list of times. It dawned on me he was showing me the times buses would be going back to Chaiyi. I thanked him to let him know I understood.

I tried to ignore Agent Collins as he climbed off the bus behind me. The trees in the park next to the parking lot were tall, with branches hanging limply in the cool, damp air. I pulled my arms further in the sleeves of my sweatshirt and headed into the streets of Guanziling. A few minutes later, I found someone sitting in front of a shop peeling some sort of fruit. I opened my guidebook and pointed at 'Fire Water Cave.' "Do you know where this is?"

She shook her head and made a gesture that she didn't understand me. I stepped closer to put my guidebook under her nose, but she pushed my hand away, saying something and shaking her head. Tears formed, and I willed myself not to cry. I'd have to call Blake already.

A young couple approached before I could get my phone out. "Can I help?" the young woman asked.

I sighed, the tension in my back melting through my body before it exited into the cement under my feet. "I want to get to the Fire Water Cave."

"Oh, it is long way. You probably should take bus."

"Where do I find a bus?" I asked.

She told me about another place to catch a bus to the cave.

She smiled as we parted. "It is up main road." she pointed to the road I had walked from the park.

"Thank you." I let out a long breath. "Xie xie," I repeated in Chinese.

"Bye bye," she said, in the way I had heard many Taiwanese people say.

"Bye bye," I returned and waved.

I stared out the window as the bus wound its way on the mountain roads. A light mist with clouds covering the ground gave the hills and mountains around me a mystical appearance.

The bus stopped, and the driver made eye contact with me and pointed to a sign that said Fire Water Cave under the Chinese characters. I climbed off. Cement stairs right in front of the bus stop led the way through an opening in a long cement wall. I hurried up the steps, excited to see the cave. People congregating around a little pond caught my attention. I almost laughed when I looked past them and saw flames climbing the rock wall behind the pond. There must have been some mistake in translation because I saw fire and water, but not any kind of cave. Flames of fire started up and extinguished randomly. Bigger flames with a constant glow skirted up the side of the cliff.

The swelling in my chest came back. It expanded until tears wet my eyes. I had made it here. The attraction left a little to be desired, but I could take care of myself.

I noticed a man step from the crowd and make his way toward a wall. He was noticeably not Taiwanese. He removed his hat, and our eyes met.

Agent Collins.

He gave a slight nod, then looked away, feigning interest in the dragon mosaic on the wall beside him. Disappointment crept up my chest. I hadn't seen him on the bus up here. I knew Agent Collins' presence was necessary, but I wished I was truly alone.

The wannabe cave didn't take long to see. I would have to find something else to do while in Chaiyi. I walked confidently to the bus stop.

"Guanziling?" I asked when I stepped onto the next bus that stopped. The driver nodded, and I got on and paid him.

I got to the park right at 12:30 and saw the bus pull in. On the way back to Chaiyi, I scanned my guidebook for anything I might want to visit. A description of a ceramics museum jumped from the page at me.

After getting off the bus, I followed the map in the guidebook until I found the museum. There was a pond with lily pads, and I walked towards it. I found a little bench and sat down to rest for a bit. I had already done more walking than I was used to, though I felt stronger than when I hiked up to the Big Buddha with Anthony and Emma. My eyelids closed and I focused on relaxing each part of my body, starting with my feet. My relaxation technique was to my arms when I heard someone speaking Chinese behind me, almost in my ear.

I jerked my head around and found myself almost face-to-face with a scrawny Taiwanese man. I jumped and scooted away on the bench. He repeated whatever he had said. I was slightly distracted by his yellow-stained teeth. He was missing a few.

I shook my head, my heart still pounding at his closeness. "I don't speak Chinese."

He stopped for a minute. He stared at me, looking awfully confused. Then he spoke again. I wished Blake were with me as I repeated myself, "I'm sorry. I don't speak Chinese."

He cocked his head and stared for a minute, and then he started pacing. He started speaking again, only this time, he was speaking louder. I cringed as his closeness enveloped me, making it hard to breathe.

The man was not giving up, so I pushed to my feet, "I'm sorry. I don't speak Chinese." Then, before he had a chance to say something else, I hurried from the pond to the museum. Before I went in, I looked back at the bench. The man was sitting where I had been. I shrugged, my heart rate slowing, and my breathing steadied. Maybe that was his bench. I caught sight of Agent Collins leaning against the far corner of the museum, texting and looking remarkably like he belonged there, white skin and all.

The museum was mostly deserted. I passed an older couple on my way into the second room. I wandered in and out of several connecting rooms in the ceramics museum. The silence weighed on me, and I thought I should probably leave. It wasn't safe for me to be alone. But the next room I entered stole my breath, and my fears slipped away to simmer in my unconsciousness.

In the center, there were drawings on how to make porcelain-type figures and their clothing. Surrounding the edges of the room were three-foot-tall figures, bringing those drawings to life. They were in different poses, and most had on stunning ancient Chinese garb. The details on the faces of the porcelain figures were intricate and made the figures lifelike. The clothing was varied in color from black to light blue, to red, to yellow. Most of the clothing had long, wide, flowing sleeves and had many layers. Some were in warrior-type clothing, and the figures each had some sort of headdress as well. Some wore hats; some wore crowns. The artist in me could stay in this room forever. I examined the tiny details painted on their faces. It was all so wonderful.

One with shimmering, purple-tinted, sheer fabric over a white dress caught my attention. The sleeves were covered slightly by draping purple fabric. The detail on the porcelain-type doll was intricate and flawless. I pressed my forehead against the glass to see as much of the figure as I could.

My walk to the train station filled me with pure joy. I had gone on my own, had fun, and didn't get lost. My happiness deflated a little when I stepped into the train station and remembered I had to get a ticket home without a note from

Blake. I almost called him, but stiffened my spine and marched up to the ticket counter.

"Changhua," I said to the man at the ticket counter. It was the only thing I could think of to say.

The man smiled at me. "You want to go to Changhua."

Relief rushed through me, almost causing me to slump to the floor before I caught myself. The man's smile widened and I had the feeling he was holding back a laugh.

A few minutes later, I was sitting on the train heading to my apartment.

My phone rang, startling me out of my happy thoughts.

"Hi, Luke."

"Alia. You sound happy."

"I am. I just traveled to a city in Taiwan all by myself."

"It might not be a good idea to be by yourself."

Dread seeped into my bones, pushing the content I had been enjoying out of my body. "Why?"

"Another guy came to Grace. Well, Grace insists it was the same guy, but this time he was claiming to be working on your security system and was wondering if she had the code so he could get in to work on it. Grace told him no and then threatened to call the police."

I gasped. "What happened next?"

"She doesn't remember. She woke up sometime later with a goose egg on her head."

"That's awful. She's lucky he didn't do worse."

"I know. Alia. Right now, I think you're safer in Taiwan, but I'm afraid he may track you down."

"I'm glad you told me, but I kind of wish you would have called me tomorrow so I could have enjoyed the feeling of independence for a bit longer."

"Sorry, Alia. I knew you would want to know, and I wanted to be sure you were still okay."

"I'm fine. Please check on Grace for me."

"I will. You might want to call her as well."

"Okay." I hung up, feeling depressed and guilty that I had been enjoying myself when Grace was putting her neck on the line for me. And the FBI watching my house hadn't caught the guy. I was sure Craig would have told me if they had.

Chapter 10

By the end of the first month, I was loving my students and had relaxed into a routine. I had traveled by myself and was making great strides to find my independence. At the school, watching the kids create had started a small fire in my stomach, a tickle in my chest, and a twitch in my fingers to create.

"What are you drawing, Minnie?" I asked as I crouched in front of where she sat.

"You," Minnie said.

I grinned. "Why are you drawing me?"

"'Cause you are nice and make me happy." She added a happy face to the drawing.

She was too sweet. "It's a good picture." I patted her jet-black hair cropped just below her chin and moved on to another student, feeling the love for these children expand in my chest.

These classrooms brought a feeling of home into my heart. I had the sense I was where I belonged. My breath caught as the thought came. It was true. Ever since my father died, I hadn't felt free to be me like I did when I was teaching my students. Blake was the only other one I was opening up to completely. It was liberating to forget about making sure those around me didn't see my pain for a few minutes as I focused on loving my students.

Between classes, I headed to the 7-Eleven down the street to find something to eat. Lights from the buildings lit the way as darkness had already fallen. I held the door open for another lady and her kids. A man ran down the street toward the store.

I had a moment of panic and rushed inside where there were plenty of people. Did Frank already find me? I took a deep breath and forced myself to relax. No, Craig would have told me if Frank had flown out of the country. They were watching all the international airports in the United States. It was nothing. The man was probably in a hurry. It had nothing to do with me.

I was deciding what I wanted for dinner when someone peeked around the aisle at me. My heart rate picked up, but I couldn't live in fear. Maybe it was Agent Collins, but I had to know for sure. I made my way to the end of the aisle and sped up as I got closer. I lunged around the corner and ran right into Blake.

"Whoa, Alia. What's your hurry?"

"Are you following me?" I blurted before I thought to put on my usual censor. I took a deep breath to calm my racing heart and to slow my breathing. My anger at Blake had nothing to do with him and everything to do with the intense fear coursing through my body.

Blake held up his hands. "I just wanted some dinner. These nights when we have the upper-level classes so late are hard. This is the only break we have"

I nodded. Blake and I were the only non-Taiwanese there at the moment. I had nothing to be afraid of. Unless Frank had commissioned a Taiwanese to help him. I huffed out a breath to give me something else to think about. My thoughts were rampaging out of control. I was just being paranoid. Suddenly, I was glad Blake had come. I wasn't worried about being alone in the store, but the dim streets were another story I hadn't thought about until now.

Blake waited for me to buy my food and held the door open for me.

"Thanks. And sorry I sort of freaked out on you."

"It's fine. Why were you freaking out?"

I waved a hand of dismissal. "I have a lot on my mind."

"Anything you want to share?"

Blake's eyes were on me, waiting. He would listen; I knew he would. But I wasn't ready to talk about all of this. Was I even allowed to? I sighed. I figured another call to Craig was in order.

———◆O◆———

I got my level 1 class started and wandered to the window as they wrote their homework in their communication books. I watched the cars and scooters drive past.

Across the street, a man was leaning against a building, silhouetted by the light above him. He wore a cap, and though I couldn't see him well, I had the distinct impression he was staring at me. I backed away so quickly that I bumped into my desk.

"Ouch."

The students turned to look at me, so I smiled at them.

"I accidentally bumped into my desk. Get your books out and we'll read."

Another look out the window helped me relax. The man was gone. I shook my head, determined to forget about it and focus on teaching.

When I had released the students to some free time, one of the boys, Steven, came up to my desk where I signed the students' communication books they took home to their parents. He always came up at the beginning of break to ask me a question. He gave me his cute, shy smile that warmed my heart every time it was directed at me.

"Teacher, you like English?"

I stifled a laugh and forgot about correcting his grammar. His eyes lit up. "Yes, Steven. I like English. It's the only way I can communicate with you."

"You should speak Chinese."

"But I don't know Chinese, Steven."

His grin grew bigger. "I teach you."

"You could teach me?" I repeated.

He nodded emphatically. "Then I wouldn't need to speak English."

I laughed and went back to signing books. He made every day better.

"Teacher?"

I put my pencil down and gave him my full attention. "Yes?"

He put his hands behind his back. He looked conflicted between wanting to talk to me and wanting to shy away. "Teacher, what you like to do here in Taiwan?"

"Why do you want to know?" I teased.

"I want to know." He shrugged.

"I enjoy spending time with the other teachers and traveling," I told him. "I like talking to you," I added. The biggest smile spread across his rounded face, and my heart melted.

Ivy, Emily, and Elaine congregated around my desk. Steven, probably surrounded by too many girls for his taste, went to join the boys in a game they were playing.

Ivy took it upon herself to organize my desk. She put the papers in piles and lined them up, so they were straight. Emily took the books I signed and called out the name of the owner so they could take them home.

As I watched my students, a calm washed over me. I had found a semblance of peace here in Taiwan.

The Chinese New Year was a couple days away and Sara told us she was treating all the employees to dinner that night since there was no school for the rest of the week.

After the last of the kids left, we piled into the school van. Soon, we sat at a large, round table with a turntable in the middle. The server brought out food, some on burners and some on serving dishes, and set them on the table and we turned it so we could get what we wanted.

An orange soup came by, and I took a bowlful. The soup, that I figured was some kind of squash, tasted delicious. Some fried sweet potato squares with a dipping sauce almost passed by me as the center turned. I reached for it, but it had gone too far.

Blake grabbed the turning center and pulled it back so I could get the fried sweet potatoes.

"Thanks."

"You said I had to make sure I introduced you to all the best food. I couldn't let you miss out on that."

"Good thing you didn't," I said after I swallowed. "I would have been mad at you forever if I missed out on ever tasting one of these." I held up another piece. He had remembered that? That had been a month ago.

Blake chuckled and went back to eating. I spooned up a vegetable dish with carrots, string beans, broccoli, and bean sprouts. After guzzling my water to try to put out the fire in my mouth, I decided one bite was enough of that.

Then they brought out the fish, and I thought I would pass out. The smell assaulted me, and I scrunched my nose. My eyes watered as I breathed deeply through my mouth to hide my reaction. I didn't want to offend Sara. My stomach lurched as the smell made it through the constricted opening to my nasal passage. The spinning center of the table slowly brought the fish closer. I leaned in my chair as it passed in front of me. They had brought out the entire fish, black beady eyes and all. Everyone used the serving fork to tear some meat off the scaly body. I let it continue past.

"You don't want any fish?" Blake asked me.

"No, thank you," I squeaked, still trying to keep from throwing up.

"You came to Taiwan, which *is* an island, and you don't eat fish," he said incredulously.

I shook my head. "The smell alone is enough to turn my stomach."

"Maybe you could eat it if you held your breath." He nudged me.

"I'll remember that when they bring Nemo out to join his dad." I tried for a joking tone but failed as the offensive smells assaulted my senses.

Blake laughed. "You're pretty funny."

My smile grew bigger, and I forgot about smells. I reflected on the last month. The unrelenting pain in my chest since my dad died was no longer a daily presence. It only manifested itself when I thought of him. My whole focus wasn't on my pain. Having the children to teach had brought me out of my head and gave me someone else to focus on.

Emma, who sat on the other side of me, talked to Anthony about how great the food was and about what she wanted to do in Kaohsiung, where she had decided we needed to spend our week off of work. Anthony made eye contact, winked, and wiggled his eyebrows. I shook my head at his obvious flirtations and scanned the room to take in the other people at the restaurant.

Then I saw him.

Chapter 11

The man wore a black hoodie with the hood covering most of his face. He stood in a far corner of the restaurant, but he leaned almost casually against the wall. I felt his eyes on me. Goosebumps prickled my arms.

"You're being awfully quiet," Blake whispered.

I jumped.

Blake chuckled. "Sorry. Didn't mean to surprise you."

I forced some words past the lump in my throat. "I... I just thought I saw someone watching me." My voice caught, betraying my fear. I turned back to find the stranger, but he was gone. Dread replaced all other feelings.

Blake put his hand on my arm. "You saw someone over there?" He jutted his chin in the direction I had been looking.

"Yeah," I whispered, not wanting to attract the attention of everyone at the table.

"What did he look like?"

I shook my head. "He had on a black hoodie, but I couldn't see his face, just like the guy I saw looking at me through the window at the school."

"You've seen him before?"

"I don't know if it was the same person."

"Excuse me." Blake stood and walked around the corner. I couldn't pull my eyes back to the group I was supposed to be eating with until Blake reappeared a few minutes later.

I raised my eyebrows as he sat.

"I didn't see anyone."

For the rest of the evening, I pushed the food around on my plate, my appetite gone.

I was relieved when dinner ended.

***

"Do you want to go to Taichung early?" Emma asked. "We could do some sightseeing and get dinner before the Chinese New Year concert."

"Sounds great," I said.

Emma took out her phone and shot off a text. A few seconds later, her phone pinged. "Anthony says we'll go in a minute."

Emma sat next to me on the couch. "How are you doing? I'm sorry we haven't had the chance to talk lately."

"I'm doing lots better. As long as I'm focused on my students, I rarely think about my dad." My voice caught, and I cleared it. "I guess being busy has helped."

"I'm always here if you need someone to talk to."

"Thanks." I wished I could tell her everything. A quick call to Craig, and he had warned me not to tell anyone unless necessary yet. He didn't want the guy to get wind I was nervous, so I had conveniently forgotten to tell him I had told Blake. He gave me the number for Agent Collins in case I needed help immediately.

When we arrived in Taichung, I followed Blake and the other teachers on a bus to the botanical gardens.

Inside the building was a tropical greenhouse. We walked along a brick path lined with benches. Vines climbed poles along the side of the path and followed the bars across the ceiling, creating a plant tunnel. Beautiful bright orange flowers with broad leaves were surrounded by smaller white flowers amid more greenery. Potted, broadleaved plants on the benches added to the depth and texture of the overall look of the greenhouse. Farther along the path, the benches and poles ended, and rocks and trees lined the walkway.

The trees along the path were smaller versions of the trees I had seen by the Big Buddha. Their trunks were small, and they wove snakelike skyward for several feet before branches sprouted to reach for the light. The glass walls of the building let sunlight filter through the leaves, warming my cheeks. I turned my face toward the ceiling, relishing the warmth, and letting it warm my insides.

We reached a small rock cliff about twenty feet long. Sections jutted outward toward the path. Water flowed down the wall and fern-like plants, whose shiny leaves appeared plastic, surrounded the water. The sound of the water flowing down the rockface, and landing in the shallow pool at the foot of the cliffs soothed my fears and worries of last night. The water splashed the ferns and small-leafed vines, causing them to sway.

"I wish I brought my sketch pad," I whispered.

"You can draw?" Anthony asked.

"Um…yeah," I said. "It's why I like teaching art. It helps me relax and forget everything around me."

"A woman of many talents." Anthony put up fingers for each item as he said them." Great with kids, can draw, can finish the fitness trail." He nudged me with his arm.

Heat crept through my cheeks, but I laughed it off. "I don't know if you should include torturing myself on the fitness trail as a talent."

"True. Let me think." He put a finger to his chin, then snapped his fingers. "I've got it. You can ride your bike right next to the cars on the road and not get killed. That was one thing that scared me to death when I got here. I mean, I grew up in California, but I never rode my bike on a busy road that didn't have a sidewalk or at least a bike path, or even a shoulder."

I shuddered slightly at the memory of the first time I rode my bike to the school. "Yeah. I was scared at first that one swivel of my handlebars would end with a car sideswiping me and pulling me under the car in a matter of seconds."

"That wouldn't be good."

I smiled, grateful for his good humor.

We wandered through the gardens. I took in all the different plants. In Idaho, I'd admired the tulips and lilies my mom grew in her garden and there were plenty of pine and oak trees lining the roads, but I had never seen such a wide variety of plants. A lump formed in my throat, and I had to fight to keep tears from falling. Why couldn't I think of home without this horrible pit in my stomach?

I hurried my steps to put some distance between me and the others to get control of my emotions. I rounded a corner and nearly ran into a guy standing in the middle of the path. His head was covered in a beanie, and he had sunglasses on. I screamed and stumbled backward. The stranger took a step toward me, then stopped as footsteps echoed behind me. I whirled around.

Blake grabbed my waist and pulled me behind him. But when we both looked to where the man had been, the stranger was gone.

"What happened?" Blake asked.

My eyes darted around. "There was a man standing there. He startled me." I couldn't be sure, but with the guy moving toward me, I felt sure he didn't have good intentions.

Blake ran to the next turn and peered around the corner. After looking down the path for a minute, he came back to join me. Emma had her arm around me, and Anthony had his hand on my shoulder, offering comfort. Blake muttered something to himself.

I got my phone out and sent a text to Agent Collins. Maybe he noticed someone exiting the gardens. He had stopped near the door when we entered.

Chapter 12

Once I could breathe again, I convinced the others we didn't need to return home. I promised I would stick close to them the whole time.

We found a little restaurant to eat dinner. Emma pointed out the nearby mall, insisting that we go shopping sometime without the boys.

As soon as everyone finished their meals, the server brought out a dessert.

"You guys have to try this," Blake said. "It's one of the best things."

The dessert was shaved ice piled on a platter and topped with sweetened condensed milk, strawberry ice cream, strawberries, whipped cream, shortbread cookies, and strawberry sauce.

"This is my new favorite dessert of all time," Emma announced.

"You can also get something with only fruit and condensed milk on it," Blake said. "It's great in the summer when it's hot."

"That sounds wonderful." I dug in for another bite, and before long we were scooping the leftover juice with our spoons.

"We better get walking to the stadium." Anthony checked his watch. "The concert will be starting soon.

We did some speed walking through the streets until we came to a grassy area with trees and a path running around little ponds.

"Welcome to Taichung Park." Anthony put a hand on my back to encourage me to go in front of him as I stopped to catch my breath. "We have enough time we can probably enjoy the scenery here."

We wandered through the park around beautiful trees with wide, spreading branches and vines curving around the trunks. Some of the bigger trees had vines as thick as tree trunks falling from the branches. We circled small ponds where the water was almost completely covered with lilies.

I shivered slightly as we walked. Blake removed his coat and rested it on my shoulders.

"I don't want to take your coat," I objected. "You'll be cold."

Blake waved me off. "I'm like an oven. Plus…" He pulled his smaller jacket closer around him. "I have this."

I rolled my eyes. "I'm like a reptile. I'm only warm when it's warm outside, and I can sit on a rock. I thought Taiwan would be more tropical," I admitted softly. "I guess I figured it'd be warm year-round. I didn't bring any coats, just a jacket and sweatshirts."

Blake nudged me with his arm. "You can borrow mine any time you need."

"Thanks."

Anthony stumbled and bumped into me. His hands caught my waist, pushing me over. He landed on top of me. He grimaced. "Sorry." He helped me up and returned my purse which had flown to the ground.

I knew we were at the concert before Anthony announced we were there. Music blared from behind the walls of the open stadium. The buildings towered over us, and concrete and bricks gave the city an industrial feel. Red awnings were the only accent color amid all the gray. With the crowds pushing into the stadium, it seemed that everyone from a hundred miles away had congregated in Taichung to celebrate the Chinese New Year.

The air, though not as cold as February in Idaho, chilled me to the bone, even with Blake's coat. The intoxicating energy of the people surrounded me. Cars could barely drive down the road as people crowded into the stadium. People shouted "Happy New Year" to us, and we returned the sentiment.

A Taiwanese woman sang to a packed stadium. The stage took up half the field, and the lights were blinding. We stood in the field, the soft turf a relief for my feet after walking so much, though I wished I could sit.

The music lulled me out of my spiraling thoughts, and I danced with Emma, Blake, and Anthony. We danced to song after song, until I was sure that midnight would never come. My legs ached, and I just wanted to go home and be alone for a minute. The woman paused in her singing, and the countdown to midnight began. When we reached zero, blue and red fireworks shot out of the top of the stadium. The fireworks were big for being so close to the earth. I clapped and cheered at the bright lights. I jumped slightly at the next spectacular burst of light only to bump into Blake.

"Having fun?" He steadied me.

"Yeah."

The fire work show wasn't done, but Blake put his hand on my back and gently steered me toward the exit. A fissure of warmth spread from his touch. Anthony and Emma followed. Anthony stepped to my other side.

We were about fifty meters from the exit when everyone else decided to leave as well. I became a sardine in a crowd of thousands as they funneled through the narrow opening to the exit. People pushed against me from all sides, forcing me against Blake. Anthony was forced behind me. Bodies pressed against mine as we edged to the exit of the stadium. Even though it was an open stadium, the body odor and stale smell of smoke almost made me gag. I put my face up toward the sky, breathing in the cold night air. The act helped me feel less cramped, but it didn't smell any better. I grabbed Emma's arm, afraid we would lose her. With my free hand, I held onto Blake's shoulder and noticed the hardness of the muscles under his jacket. My breath caught in my throat and my heart did a little pitter patter.

Anthony was pressed against my back.

Even as we exited the stadium onto a smaller side street, the people still crowded me uncomfortably. Everyone talked to each other, and Blake spoke to random people in Chinese. They seemed delighted that he spoke the language.

Even with the joviality, panic flooded my body. My vision blurred, and everyone became images flowing in and out and up and down. I pointed my face to the sky and took a deep breath as a wave of nausea clogged my throat.

It wasn't until we reached the main street that the crowds thinned. I let go of Emma and Blake, relieved when my heartbeat returned to a more normal pace. I took a deep breath of the cold air to calm the tremors in my hands. Slowly the panic I had been feeling slipped into the night air with my breathing.

After we had made it home, I threw my purse on the bed. A white piece of paper slid out of the side pocket. I pulled at it and extracted an envelope. It dropped to the floor as I let go of it like it was a cockroach. I swallowed to keep from crying out and stared at the envelope. There was no writing on the outside. Where had it come from? I knew it wasn't there before since my mother had ingrained in me the need to clean out my purse every evening. I sat and the edge of my bed and slowly slit it open.

Chapter 13

I know what you have. I will get it.

My heart stopped.

A shiver went down my back. I immediately called Craig.

"Someone put a note in my purse," I said as soon as he answered.

"A note? Do you know who could've left it?"

"I have no idea." I paused. "Well, there was a guy at the botanical gardens."

"What guy?"

I quickly told him what had happened at the botanical gardens and the guy I saw at the restaurant the night before.

"Right." The way he said it made me think that none of this was new information.

"Is the guy the other FBI agent?" I asked.

"No, but Agent Collins is aware of all of this. What did the note say?"

"I know what you have. I will get it."

"And it was in an envelope?"

"Yeah."

Craig was silent so long that I wanted to babble more, but I had no incriminating evidence, so I just waited.

"It seems odd to have that short of note in an envelope."

"An envelope's stiffer," I pointed out. "It would be easier to slip in my purse without me noticing."

"Okay. Be extra cautious."

"I will. Thanks."

I curled up on my bed and fell asleep despite thoughts spinning in my head.

Someone knocking at my door startled me awake a few hours later. Emma poked her head in.

"Oh sorry. I thought you would be up by now." Emma went to close the door again.

"It's okay. You said we were going to Lugang today? When are we leaving?"

"Yeah. Blake and Anthony are already here. Do you still want to come?"

"Yes. I'll throw some clothes on."

Emma closed the door and I scrambled to put the pants that lay next to my bed on and threw on a fresh shirt. I pulled my hair into a top-knot and put a little mascara on. I almost laughed at the look of shock my dad would have if he saw me going out into public like this, but I liked it. Free to look how I wanted and not worry about what everyone would think. I liked it a lot.

When we got to Lugang, claustrophobia set in when I saw the people-filled street Emma and Anthony led us to. I stuck out in the crowd as I could see over the heads of most of the Taiwanese people wandering in and out of the shops. Not only was I tall, but my blonde hair made me stand out even more. I was suddenly jealous of Blake's dark hair and tanned skin. But the attention didn't seem to bother Anthony. I smiled at all the people I saw staring at me, unwilling to let their attention make me self-conscious.

I followed the other teachers in and out of shops, taking in all the trinkets people could buy.

"I'll be right back," Blake said as he made his way through the throng of people. I watched him over the heads of everyone packed in the street as he went to a food vendor.

He returned with a couple of bags full of thick French fries. "Sweet potato fries," he said. "Like what you had at the restaurant."

"Thanks." I munched on the fries as we continued down the street. "You're taking my challenge of making sure I try all the best food seriously."

"What good is coming to Taiwan if you don't get a chance to try all the food?" Blake nudged me, and heat rose through my neck. I blinked and pretended to take intense interest in some trinkets and hoped Blake hadn't noticed.

A few minutes later, Blake grabbed my hand and pulled me into a little shop, leaving Emma and Anthony at the shop next door where Emma was trying to decide if she wanted to buy a large round hat made out of thin pieces of wood. My hand tingled in Blake's grasp, and I commanded my erratic heartbeat to return to normal.

"I thought you might want to see this," Blake whispered.

When my eyes adjusted to the interior of the shop, my eyes drifted to the displays on the walls. My breath whooshed out of my lungs leaving me a little lightheaded. The wall was lined with intricately hand-painted fans.

"Wow," I whispered. A detailed picture depicting different scenes adorned each fan. A garden, a building, the beach. My eyes darted from one fan to the other, taking it all in.

"He paints them." Blake nodded toward the gentleman standing behind the counter.

"You like?" he asked.

"I love them."

Blake spoke some Chinese with the man, then came back to where I stood. "These are some pictures he can paint for you."

I gaped at him. " I didn't bring any money."

"You pay him when he brings it to you, or when you pick it up."

"He'll bring it to me?"

"He did for me." Blake shrugged.

"You have one of these?" I was in a stupor. Blake had found my weak spot.

Blake chuckled. "Yeah."

I took the little binder full of pictures and rifled through them.

"I'm going to go tell Anthony and Emma where we are. I'll be right back." Blake left the shop.

I closed the book. I didn't want one of these generic pictures. I wanted something that would remind me of my parents. But I hadn't really drawn anything substantial since my dad's death. I looked up at the artist, determined. "Do you have paper and a pen or pencil?"

I glanced around to see if Blake had returned. He was standing outside the shop. I hoped he wouldn't come in soon. I didn't know if I could do what I was planning with him looking over my shoulder.

The fan artist cocked his head at me quizzically for a moment and then retrieved a sheet of paper from under the counter and gave me a pen.

I studied the fans around me. I started with an outline of my dad leading a horse I was riding before he released the horse and let me ride across the corral. I sketched my mom and I lounging on the back patio, enjoying the flower gardens my mom loved so much. Above the pictures in bubbly, flowing script I wrote "Find Yourself." Those were the words my mom told me before she died. I needed to find myself, and I knew I was on my way to doing just that. I added a few more pictures of things that reminded me of my parents. I wondered how I could let him know what colors to use but didn't worry about it. I drew the figures of my parents on the front step.

Tears welled in my eyes, and I stood up straight to keep the tears from falling on the picture. I blinked and went back to work, telling myself I could cry later. The people in my drawing didn't have details, but I knew who they were and that was all that mattered.

I finished the sketch, stretching my back while figuring out how to show him the color.

His eyes shone with admiration. "You are talented."

I ducked my head, slightly embarrassed at his praise. "I'd like it in color."

"One moment." He produced some colored pencils. "I draw pictures on paper before painting on fan."

I added color to my drawing, blending colors the best I could. I handed him the picture when I finished.

"I've never done anything like this," he said.

"Please," I said, tears wetting my eyes.

He nodded vigorously. "No problem. I can do it."

"Thank you! I'll come pick it up." I turned around and bumped into Blake. I wondered how long he had been standing there. It was easy to lose track of time while I drew.

"No, no," the man said. "I bring it to you. Where at?"

Blake answered in Chinese then grinned at me. "Did you draw a picture for him to paint on your fan?"

I blushed and was grateful for the dark interior. "Um, yeah. Did you find Emma and Anthony?"

"They are a few shops down the road." He gestured for me to go in front of him through the opening. "I can't wait to see what you came up with."

"I'd like to see your fan."

A shiver went up my back as we stepped into the sunshine. It wasn't the thrilling shiver that came from Blake's touch. This shiver left me cold with a feeling of foreboding. I scanned the crowded street. There were so many people, but that feeling stopped me in my tracks. There was someone across the street, fiddling with some trinkets in a shop. He had sunglasses, and a ballcap shadowed his face, but blond hair stuck out from under his hat. He had long pants and a long-sleeved shirt on, which wasn't totally out of the ordinary. I squinted at him.

Chapter 14

"Alia?"

I jumped at Blake's question. He stared at me with concern.

"Sorry, what were you saying?" I glanced across the street, but just like the other night, the man had disappeared.

"I was just telling you I'd show you my fan when we get back."

"That'd be great." I continued to search for the stranger, but he had vanished into the crowds.

"What is it?" Blake asked.

I opened my mouth to tell Blake about the guy but stopped myself. I had two agents watching me. They would take care of things.

"Nothing." I made my way over to Anthony and Emma.

As we walked home from the bus stop, we discussed our trip to Kaohsiung.

"You ready to go on vacation tomorrow?" Anthony asked me.

"Yeah. I hope you guys have some awesome things for us to see," I said.

"You bet. We're going to see Cijin Island and probably swim at Kenting. And we definitely can't miss Monkey Mountain." Emma ticked off her fingers as she named the places we would visit. My stomach tingled at the idea of doing more sightseeing. I was also anxious to forget about the guy I had seen several times now in as many days. There was no way the guy would know our plans.

When we got back to our apartment, Blake stopped me. "I want to show you that fan I told you about."

"I'll see you later." Emma wiggled her eyebrows, so I rolled my eyes. I hadn't even told my roommate the effect Blake had on me, but she knew.

I followed Blake into his apartment and sat down on their couch. Blake went into his room to get the fan. Anthony sat on the couch next to me, his arm draped around my shoulder. I leaned forward, not wanting Anthony to feel like he could get too friendly.

Blake rejoined me in the living room and handed his fan to me. I opened it carefully and the picture on it nearly took my breath away. There, beautifully depicted on the stiff, though almost transparent, paper, was the Idaho Falls Temple. Memories came flooding back: walking the greenbelt with my parents, admiring the temple over the falls. I had spent hours in that spot waiting for the exact moment to take a picture at sunset so I could then paint the picture for my parents. It still hung in their bedroom. It was one of the works I was most proud of. I took a deep breath to keep the flood of emotions from overwhelming me.

"What is it?" Anthony asked. "It's beautiful. And when did you get it? You've only been here a month."

"I got it while I was here for my mission."

"It's the Idaho Falls Temple," I said almost at the same time turning to Anthony. "It's a special place in our religion." The fan was a true work of art. "It's beautiful," I breathed.

The guy was very talented. I knew he would do my picture justice. Excitement bubbled inside me, but it was tempered by the thought of what the picture showed. It showed that everything I had valued at home was gone, and I needed a picture to remember it. I swallowed. This place, beautifully depicted on the fan, reminded me I would see my parents again, but even that thought was no comfort as a crushing grief gripped me.

My throat tightened, and I knew I couldn't keep the tears from falling anymore. I excused myself and hurried across the hall to my apartment.

Emma stared when I burst through the front door and ran to my room. After frantically looking around for anything to help ease the emotions, I grabbed my sketch pad and charcoal and bolted out of the apartment. I needed to be alone. The elevator doors were closing when Emma called, "Alia, wait!"

I didn't wait. I hurried to a long, narrow pond surrounded by trees that bordered the University campus. I found a place to sit that had a good view of the lily pads in the pond and showed a red-arched bridge going over the narrow end. The trees reached to the sky at the same time their branches fell to the earth. I stared at my sketchbook for a moment as I sat on a rock next to the pond. I had grabbed them out of habit. Until recently, drawing had always helped me figure out my thoughts. Drawing hadn't killed me today. In fact, for that brief moment, it had made me feel close to my parents.

I took a deep breath and started sketching. I drew the bridge and the pond, working on relaxing my grip to keep the lines rounded and flowing as my emotions threatened to take over. Concentrating on the serenity before me helped, and the picture became easier to draw. The lines started flowing from me and I started blending—a forgotten part of me rearing back to life.

Art was a part of me. I was adding details on the bridge when I sensed someone watching me. Fear coursed through my veins, making my hands tremble. Had the strange man found me here? I didn't want to be caught alone. Glancing around for Agent Collins, I saw Emma who stood a few feet behind me. I breathed a sigh of relief.

"That's awesome." She gestured to my sketch pad. "I knew you liked teaching art, but I have never seen you draw, and I've been living with you for a month."

"I thought my passion died with my dad, but with all the turmoil going on inside me, it was second nature."

"Blake said you drew a picture for the guy to paint on a fan."

"I almost stopped myself, but I wanted a fan that meant something to me, not just a generic picture."

Emma put her hand on my shoulder. "Alia. It's okay to miss your dad and do things for you. I can see that art is a big part of who you are. Don't let a part of you die with him"

"But I don't want him dead." I glanced at the scene I had been drawing, trying to find the serenity inside of me that I saw here. "I miss him…and my mom."

"I know. A part of you will probably always be sad that they are gone. You can miss them and be sad they are gone, but you are still here and shouldn't punish yourself. It just makes you more miserable and spiteful." Emma blinked rapidly, and I realized I didn't know much about her. Our conversations thus far had been pretty surface-level.

"You sound like you know."

"My sister and mother were killed in a car accident when I was a Senior in high school."

I gasped. "Oh, Emma. That's awful."

"I was mad at my dad for letting them go." She shook her head. "In my grief, I wanted to blame someone. But it's not like my dad knew they were going to die." She gazed out over the lily-covered water.

I wondered if a part of her still blamed her dad. I didn't want to press her, though.

Emma took a deep breath and continued. "Maybe most of the crying has been because you have been angry. Or because you feel shame because you think it was your fault somehow." She paused for a moment. "I know I felt that way, no matter how illogical it was. I should have stopped them from going. I should have faked sickness, so my mom would have stayed home." She took another deep breath. "Maybe now, you need to let yourself miss them without hiding your emotions."

The wall around my heart crumbled. My body shook as it let out the emotions I had been keeping in for so long. Emma wrapped her arms around my shoulders and hugged me, letting me cry. When the tears subsided, I felt hallow but strangely cleansed.

"Better?" Emma asked.

I nodded, amazed.

Emma gave me a squeeze before we got up and made our way back to the apartment. We needed to pack for our trip, but I felt that my friendship with Emma had grown stronger. I was glad she had shared a part of herself with me. I would have never guessed she knew the pain I felt since she always acted happy and excited to live life.

Chapter 15

"Craig, I saw some guy watching me again," I whispered into my phone to keep Emma from hearing. I had been so overcome with emotion the night before I decided to get up early before we left Kaohsiung.

"Where?"

"Lugang." I paused before I voiced the concern I had been grappling with. "How did he know I would be there?"

"Are you sure it's the same person?"

"No. Am I just being paranoid?"

"I'm not sure, Alia."

"He must be watching the apartment and following me somehow," I said.

"If it is the same person you saw at the restaurant and at the gardens, it wouldn't be hard to note what bus you left on, then ask where that bus was headed," Craig added.

"We're going to Kaohsiung today. We're leaving pretty early, though."

"Promise you will always have someone with you. This guy may be waiting for you to go somewhere alone. And you let me know if he ever makes a threatening move."

The intensity in his voice stunned me. For a moment, I couldn't find any words. I opened my mouth several times to say something, but the fissure of fear I felt when I thought the stalker had found me alone the night before was something I didn't want to ignore.

"I'll make sure someone is with me," I promised, then I ended the call and started packing.

We arrived in Kaohsiung after a three-hour train ride. I yearned to experience more of the culture. I had been amused by the houses in the middle of rice fields. I assumed they were farmhouses, but like everything else in Taiwan, were built straight up. Even though there were no other buildings connected, they were three stories high and almost perfectly square. Odd colors adorned each of the walls, as if the builders couldn't decide what color to paint it so they had gone with three of their favorites, one of them being gray.

Despite the beauty that lay before me, I missed houses that sprawled out, taking up space without abandon. I squeezed my eyes shut. I missed home and living on the outskirts of the city.

When we made it to Kaohsiung and were walking down a road surrounded by buildings towering above me, Blake broke the silence. "You've been really quiet. A penny for your thoughts?"

"I was just thinking about home."

"Do you miss it?" he asked.

I shrugged. "Yeah, but I miss my dad more, but he isn't there."

"I'm sorry." Blake took my hand in his and gave it a squeeze. He held on for a moment longer than I would have expected before letting go. A thrill ran through my body and made my legs wobbly enough that I had to grab onto Blake's arm for support. His warm hand covered mine, and I didn't bother taking my hand back. For the first time, I felt a deep longing to remain close to someone.

We turned up a little alleyway barely wide enough for one car to drive through. A few steps led to each door of this residential area. There were no awning storefronts, just stairs, doors, and single garage openings. The second door had a sign that said, OUR FRIEND'S HOUSE.

"This is our home for the next few days." Blake opened the door for us.

Emma stepped into the building. "Thanks for booking this for us. I've enjoyed having someone around who can speak the language. It's a lot more convenient than asking Sara."

The lady who owned the hostel took our payment for five nights, and we went to the third floor where there were two bedrooms. One was labeled *women* and the other was labeled *men*. I took my stuff into the girls' room with Emma. There were three bunks on either side of the room. A window on the opposite wall let natural light in between the two lines of beds. I chose a bunk next to the window, and Emma chose the bunk on top of mine.

An hour later, after we had eaten lunch, we went to the metro station. We waited for travelers to exit the train before the throng of people wanting to get into the cars pushed us in. We stood at the center of the car, Emma and I holding onto a vertical pole and Blake and Anthony grabbing a bar above their heads. The car was so full that people jostled against me constantly.

After walking a half-mile from another metro station, my legs shook, and my heart hammered against my chest. I fell gratefully onto a seat on the ferry.

I scanned the island as we got closer. A small lighthouse stood on a bluff on the right, acting like a beacon of the potential this trip held for me. It was perfect for a picture. I reached for my phone to snap a picture, but it wasn't in my pocket. I checked my purse, but it wasn't there. I must have left it at the hostel. I would have to rely on my memory.

Blake held onto my elbow and helped me to the stairs to exit. His grip steadied me as the ferry continued to tip back and forth.

Unfortunately, the lighthouse was closed, but Emma didn't let that get her down, and she headed toward Cihou Fort. My legs may be stronger than a month ago, but after all the walking we had already done, I was getting tired. I ignored my heavy breathing as the hike didn't seem to affect my friends at all. The fort itself consisted of concrete and red brick. Concrete tunnel entrances opened every hundred feet or so up the side of the hill. Dirt and shrubbery surrounded the openings.

Emma pointed to a sign near the entrance of the top of the fort and dragged Blake over to translate it for her.

"Come on, I want to see the view." Anthony lightly nudged me forward. I wasn't particularly interested in reading the signs, so I was grateful for the distraction.

I closed my eyes for a moment as the breeze from the sea cooled my flushed cheeks. I turned to say something about the beauty to Anthony, but I was alone.

Panic rose in my chest, and I scanned the upper part of the fort. My gaze landed on a man leaning against the red-bricked arch that led to another part of the fort. There was no denying who it was now. He had his hat on, but I could clearly see his face and he was staring at me.

It was the man from the cemetery. His dark eyes sent shivers down my spine, even from this distance. His lips curled into a smirk, and he pushed from the wall. I took a few staggering steps backward, scanning the area for a means of escape.

"Alia?" Blake called from behind me.

I almost slumped to the floor. I turned on shaking legs to see him running toward me. I grabbed onto his arm as he came up beside me. I searched for the nameless stranger again, but he had disappeared.

Blake grabbed my arm to support me and searched my face with his blue eyes then scanned the area. "Where is Anthony? I thought he was with you."

I took a shaky breath and shrugged. "I saw the guy who I think is following me."

Blake again scanned the area. "Is he still around?"

"I don't know where he went." My eyes swept the area, hoping I could point him out.

"Stick close to me, will you?" Blake led me past the small concrete rooms forming the perimeter of the top of the fort to an outside wall that afforded us the view of the island to our left and the sea out in front of us and to our right.

I hadn't planned on being alone in the first place. I gripped Blake's bicep, and my breath caught when I felt the flexed muscle under my touch. I began to relax in Blake's presence, feeling safe and secure with him nearby.

I gazed across the island, where buildings clustered on this tiny strip of land, glinting pale green, red, and tan in the waning sunlight. The beach bordered the southern shore, and people, only tiny specks from this height, dotted the sandy strip of land. The breeze blew a few stray hairs in front of my face, and I turned to savor the coolness of the wind, reassured by Blake's arm under my hand.

"Alia?" Blake's voice sounded hoarse, so I opened my eyes. His blue eyes showed a strange depth I had never seen before. He brushed a strand of hair out of my face. My breath caught, and Blake's throat moved as if swallowing hard.

"There you are," Anthony said.

Blake pulled his hand away.

Anthony glanced at Blake before speaking to me. "I went to see another part of the fort and thought you were right behind me. When I turned around you were gone."

"I was enjoying the sea breeze and when I opened my eyes, I couldn't find you."

"I'm sorry. I didn't mean to lose you."

Emma stepped on the platform. "Wow. This is a great view. Blake, can you come translate another sign?"

Blake's eyes shifted from me to Anthony.

"I'll be fine." I mouthed. After a hesitant nod, he followed Emma, but he kept me in his view.

Grateful for the distance, I tried to make sense of what had just happened. I couldn't deny the physical attraction I had, but this was the first glimpse I'd caught that Blake maybe felt it too. I turned to face the sea, thinking it would distract me from the lump in my throat.

Anthony stared at me for so long that a strange trepidation ran through my body. I brought my hand to my hair to try to tame it in the breeze.

I couldn't take his scrutiny any longer. "What?"

"Nothing. Sorry. I just… don't really know what to make of you, you know?"

I raised an eyebrow at him. "No, I don't think I do."

"I mean, I…" He stopped and cleared his throat. "Never mind."

I pivoted to look over the island to give me some time to compose myself, confusion clouding my thoughts. I stuffed my hands into my jacket pocket. One hand collided with stiff folds of paper. I turned so Anthony wouldn't be able to see and pulled the paper out enough to get a glimpse of it. I gasped and shoved it into my pocket.

Anthony's hand rested on my shoulder. "What's wrong?"

"Nothing," I said, forcing my voice to not betray the nerves bouncing in my chest. It was another envelope, just like the one I'd found in my purse after the concert a couple of days ago. I wanted to run and find somewhere secluded to look at it, but after seeing the stalker, I didn't dare go anywhere alone. I took a deep breath to calm the rapid beats exploding in my chest.

Anthony studied me for a moment so I didn't think he believed me.

I took a slow deep breath. I would find some time alone to read it. Now that I knew for sure who the man was, I didn't want to be alone anywhere except in the hostel.

Chapter 16

Blake and Emma waved from the entrance a couple of yards away, so I hurried to join them, aware of Anthony trailing behind me.

"Well, what do you say we head down the hill to explore more of the island?" Emma nearly skipped down the path before the rest of us had a chance to answer.

Emma led us through a tunnel that exited onto a sort of concrete pier that extended into the ocean with slabs jutting out into the sea, probably to let boats dock. It went straight into the ocean for about half a mile. People stood around the tunnel opening, and I could even see a few at the end of the pier.

"Do you want to walk out there?" Blake asked.

"Of course," Emma said.

I took a deep breath as I stepped on the pier. The sea on both sides made me jittery, which only compounded the nervousness from seeing the guy from the cemetery. I wanted to run somewhere for some privacy. I felt sure he was just waiting for me to be alone to act. I looked around to be sure he hadn't followed us. But I didn't see anyone interested in watching me. The sun was in its descent, but I could tell we still had plenty of daylight. I squinted to see the end of the pier, but the light reflecting off the water made it hard to focus.

We were about halfway down the pier when we came to a group of young Taiwanese guys. They stopped us, and one's eyes zeroed in on me. "We get picture with you?"

"Why do you want a picture with me?" I asked nervously. I studied each one, searching for any sign of mal intent.

"We like getting pictures with a beautiful American," another said.

I ducked my head at their compliment. It wasn't a sentiment that was foreign to me, but I didn't like the extra attention.

I glanced at Blake and Anthony. They wouldn't let me be abducted. Anthony gave me a reassuring nod.

"I guess," I relented.

One guy asked Anthony to take the picture. The guys crowded around me. My stomach clenched, and my muscles tightened. I couldn't understand why I wanted to run. I chalked it up to seeing the guy on the fort. I suddenly felt any stranger was danger.

I posed for the picture but knew fear showed on my face. The Taiwanese guys waved for Emma to join us and I relaxed marginally having her near. My friends bid the Taiwanese guys farewell while I did a half-hearted wave.

Blake stepped up beside me. "They mean no harm. Can you blame them for wanting a picture with you?"

My chest tightened. "Are you mocking me?"

His face grew serious. "I'm not mocking you. You're beautiful, funny, nice."

"Thanks," I said. "I'm just nervous because of that guy."

"What guy?" Emma asked.

"I've seen a guy three times over as many days and he's starting to make me anxious."

"What? Why didn't you tell me?" Emma threw her arms around me.

"I thought I was being paranoid." I took a deep breath. "It would help if we stayed together."

"For sure," Emma said.

Blake grabbed my hand, and we made our way to the end of the pier. Blake's touch helped my fears slowly slip away. As long as I kept Blake near, I didn't have to fear the stranger. I was certain Blake, and even Anthony, would help me. I just had to stick close to them until I could report the latest events to Craig.

The pier narrowed slightly at the end. I sat down in the center, pulling Blake beside me, and breathed deeply. I closed my eyes, and after a moment, the sound of waves lapping against the shore calmed my nerves.

Blake gave my hand a squeeze then let go. A sense of loss enveloped me, but I focused on the beauty in front of me. The few clouds in the eastern sky were starting to turn pink as the sun neared the horizon. We sat silently, each of us lost in our own thoughts. Out in the distance, I could see the faint outlines of some larger boats.

"Let's head back." Blake stood and offered to help me up.

My heart hummed in anticipation as I reached for his hand, then raced forward, and my breath caught. I smiled at him before breaking contact and folding my arms against the chill in the air. Uncertainty flared through me. What was I going to do about my feelings for Blake? I had barely a glimpse that he might feel the same, so I didn't want to throw myself at him. I would wait patiently until he made another move.

We enjoyed the ocean breeze as we strolled to the island. The loss of solitude when we started passing people carved a small pit in my stomach. We found our way to the beach on the opposite side of the island, only a half mile from where the ferry had dropped us off. I stared at the sea from the beach.

"Look at that sunset." I sighed. The sun touched the horizon, right next to the hill that supported the fort. Beautiful shades of orange and red lit up the mini cliffs and reflected off the water and spray of the sea.

I sat on the sand and stared at the beauty around me, almost forgetting my friends were there. Suddenly there were tears in my eyes.

"You okay?" Blake asked from beside me.

I gave him a small smile, surprised I didn't feel sad or embarrassed.

"I just feel so happy and at peace right now."

"Why is that?"

"I'm not sure." Tears splattered my cheeks as the realization hit me. "I used to watch the sunset with my parents on warm summer nights. We would sit on the front porch, not saying anything, but enjoying each other's company." I glanced up at him. " I know it sounds a little odd to be thinking of that when I'm so far away from home."

Blake put his arm around me and pulled me close. "I don't think it is odd. You are seeing a beautiful sunset here like you did there." His voice lowered to a whisper. "I'm glad I'm getting the chance to know you."

My heart thumped as I raised my eyes to meet his. He gave my shoulders a squeeze.

"Let's head back," Anthony said, glancing at me and Blake.

I stood up and brushed the sand off my pants, slightly embarrassed that Anthony and Emma had witnessed the intimate moment between me and Blake.

We walked down the short, wide street between the beach and the ferry. The music and lights were a sharp contrast to the serenity of the beach. It appeared to be a carnival with game and food booths. Maybe it was a Chinese New Year's Party.

Blake went to one booth and came back with four mini, round cakes to share.

I studied it." I've seen these before. They look like they have red mud in the middle." I eyed him suspiciously.

"Trust me," Blake said.

I did trust him. I trusted him to protect me from a guy who was following me around the island. What I didn't trust were my growing feelings. I took a tentative bite and was pleasantly surprised. The middle was filled with a sort of vanilla cream pudding.

"That was delicious, Blake. Thanks!" Emma said, finishing her last bite.

Soon we were on the ferry riding toward tiny dots of light on top of gently rolling waves. The ferry pulled up to its port back at Kaohsiung, and we headed to the stairs. We were almost out of the crowd when Emma screamed.

"Hey!" She ran after someone carrying her purse, and Blake sprinted after her. Anthony and I hurried after them, but the crowd swallowed them. I paused, panting.

"Which way did they go?" I asked.

"I don't know. Let's see if we can find them." Anthony placed his hand on my back and led me from the ferry in the direction we last saw Blake and Emma running.

Afraid of losing Blake and Emma, I sprinted several blocks through the darkened streets. Confident Anthony was right behind me, I crossed one street and then another.

"Maybe we should go to the ferry and wait for them to find us," I suggested.

No answer. Anthony was gone. I backtracked to the street I had crossed, but there was no sign of him. It was then I realized I couldn't even hear the noise of the crowd at the ferry. How far had we gone?

I tried calling out, but my throat constricted. I could barely breathe. I had to find my way to the ferry. I searched every side road as I hurried down the street in what I hoped was the right direction.

There were no streetlights to light my way. *It's okay.* I told myself to calm my racing heart. *It's so dark the stalker won't be able to see you either. You just have to get to the ferry.*

The thought of the guy from the cemetery stopped me in my tracks.

"Anthony?" I tentatively called. No answer.

I retraced my steps the best I could, but we had turned so many times I wasn't sure where the ferry was. I was on a small side street, and the dark buildings hovering above me pressed their shadows onto my chest. My eyes darted from one building to the next, searching for anywhere the stalker might be able to hide.

After wandering for ten minutes, doubt crowded my thoughts until my feet finally stopped. I was lost. I glanced behind me, then took a few more tentative steps forward. A figure appeared down the street. I ducked into the shadows and held my breath as the person passed by. Panicked, I moved my long legs as fast as I could across the road and turned right, away from the lone person. I needed to call Blake. I reached for my back pocket. Then I remembered I didn't have my phone. A fresh wave of adrenaline shot through my body.

The darkness pressed down on me as I passed a section of closed businesses.

My breath sounded raspy, even to me. My heart beat loudly in my chest, and I could feel the blood pulsing in my neck. Someone would have realized I was not at the ferry by now. I stared at the street, trying to remember how far I had come before I turned onto this road. Maybe I should hunker down here and wait for someone to find me.

Pounding footsteps echoed behind me. I glanced behind me. A tall man ran toward me. Panic shot through me and I sprinted away. The person was gaining, fast. Two arms wrapped around me and pulled me off my feet.

Chapter 17

I screamed and pushed, but my captor hoisted me over his shoulder and ran down a small side street. The man behind me shouted and I shrieked. The person carrying me stumbled forward, but I could tell I was slowing him down. I kicked and flailed. My captor cursed—in English. The shoulder under me jostled as if he'd tripped, and I fell to the ground landing hard on my hip. The person behind us passed. I scrambled to my feet and attempted to limp away. My chest constricted, and I struggled to breathe.

"Alia, wait." Someone grabbed my shoulder. The blood rushing through my ears made it so I could hardly hear.

My vision blurred, and blackness enclosed around me. I tried to fight it. What would happen to me if I passed out? My legs gave way, but the unknown man caught me and lifted me into his arms.

"Alia, I'm sorry. I lost him."

"Blake?" I asked.

"Are you okay?" he asked, still carrying me.

I rested my head against his shoulder as he carried me down the street. When he adjusted me in his arms a third time, I said, "I think I'm strong enough to walk."

Blake set me down, his hand tense on my back. "Are you sure?"

"Yeah," I said, then the world started to spin. I moved to sit, but Blake held me up, probably afraid I was passing out.

"Let me sit a minute." He eased me onto my hands and knees. The grime on the street coated my palms. The gritty feeling clung to every part of me, but I had no choice. My breathing was ragged, and I didn't know what was happening.

I spoke, hoping voicing my thoughts would help me make sense of the events of the past few minutes. "One minute someone was behind me chasing me, but then someone caught me, but they were running from the person behind me." My whole body shook. My arms threatened to collapse under me, so I turned and sat down, cringing slightly at the thought of the filth I might be sitting on. My eyes were still flitting from Blake to where I wanted to run. Everything inside of me wanted to bolt.

Had Blake been chasing me?

"I'm sorry, Alia, I didn't mean to scare you. I called to you, but you must not have heard me." The sound of Blake's voice forced me to meet his gaze. He was crouched in front of me. He looked nervous, scared even.

My hand went to my mouth to calm myself. I felt the grit on my face and wiped my hand on my shirt.

"Alia. I was the one behind you. I saw you turn and tried to get your attention since you were going the wrong way. Then I saw that guy grab you." He moved as though he were going to touch my face but stopped. "Alia, I was so scared."

Head between my knees, I concentrated on taking slow deep breaths. I repeated over and over that I was safe, now.

I jumped when he put a hand on my arm. "The thief dropped Emma's purse. Anthony said he lost track of you. I thought I'd walk around, see if I'd run into you while they waited at the ferry." He paused and almost whispered, "I didn't mean to scare you. I'd...I would never hurt you."

I could hear confusion and pain in his voice. "I'm sorry," I choked out. "I didn't realize it was you."

"Alia..." Blake sat next to me. "You don't need to be sorry."

I shook my head. "But who was that other guy?"

Blake put an arm around my shoulders. "I don't know, but he's long gone."

I continued to breathe slowly to get rid of the fear that gripped my chest. "It was probably the same person who I saw at the fort. I saw him..." I cut myself off. Should I be telling Blake all of this? As long as I didn't tell him the FBI was here watching me, it should be okay. I started again. "I think he may be the same person I saw in Lugang, and..."

"What?" Blake said. "Do you think it is the same person who was at the restaurant and at the gardens?"

"Maybe. I didn't get a good look at him before today. Then there are the strange notes."

"What notes?"

I waved my hand. "Nothing."

"No, it's not nothing."

Blake rested an arm around me. He put his lips right next to my ear. "Please, Alia. Tell me what's going on."

I turned to him, my cheek brushing against his nose. "I don't know," I cried. "But I'm scared."

His arm tightened, and he cupped my chin, turning my face to his. "It's okay, Alia. You're safe. I wouldn't let anything happen to you."

I debated for a moment. Maybe it wouldn't hurt for him to know about the notes. "I found an envelope in my purse after the concert the other night. It had a note inside saying that they know what I have and that they are going to get it."

"What do you have?"

I didn't answer, and Blake didn't press me for one. I didn't want to tell anyone about the money. It was supposedly safe in different accounts, but if this man kidnapped me, then would he be able to torture the information out of me?

We sat there for several minutes. Blake held me with one arm until I finally felt I could walk.

"Let's go. I need to lie down," I said. My stomach inched uncomfortably close to my mouth, and I definitely did not want to throw up in front of Blake. He stood and helped me up, then held my elbows as if to ascertain that I really could walk

He put his arm around my waist as I limped along. "You said notes, plural. What did the others say?"

"I haven't read it yet. I don't even know if it is a note for sure." I pulled out the folded piece of paper from my pocket. "I don't know how it got there."

Blake gently pulled me to a stop. "You received it today?"

"Well, I assume it was today. I didn't notice it before."

"Why didn't you say something?"

"I wanted to know what it said before I showed it to anyone."

"May I see it when we get back to the hostel?"

"Sure." I slipped it back into my pocket.

He kept his arm around me all the way to the ferry. I leaned into him, letting him support and comfort me. When we met up with Emma and Anthony, the tears fell again as Emma wrapped her arms around me.

"I'm sorry I lost you, Alia." Anthony rested his hand on me. "I thought I saw Blake down a street we passed. By the time I figured out it wasn't him, you were gone. I should have called after you."

"It's in the past now." I didn't want Anthony to feel too badly.

When we got to the hostel, Blake hurried with me up the stairs.

Tremors shook my whole body by the time I reached the top of the stairs, and I paused for a moment, holding onto the banister, deciding if I trusted my legs.

Blake slipped his arm around my waist and helped me to the girl's room.

After making sure no one was sleeping inside, he turned on the light and led me to my bed. I was grateful Anthony and Emma didn't follow us in, since I was not sure I wanted more than Blake with me when I read the note. I sat down on something hard—my phone. I had probably tossed it there and forgot to put it in my pocket.

I took a deep breath, tore open the envelope, and pulled out a single piece of paper.

Your father's death wasn't an accident.

A tear slipped down my cheek. If he knew that, did that mean he meant for me to endure the same fate?

"What does it say?" Blake sat next to me.

I felt like throwing up, so I put a hand to my mouth and held out the note.

"Alia. This is serious. We should tell the police."

"But the police here have no jurisdiction over where my dad died."

"No, but they have jurisdiction over whoever is tormenting you."

"You're right. But can it wait until morning? I'm so tired." I knew I wouldn't be able to call the police, but Blake could do it for me.

Blake clasped my hand. "Alia. I'm sorry I didn't catch him tonight. He turned a corner, and he was gone."

"That seems to be his specialty."

Blake put his arm around me. "I thought tonight was a fluke, but I'm even more worried knowing someone's been delivering notes onto your person. Who can get close enough to do that?"

I shrugged. "I was surrounded by people on the metro and on the ferry."

"We'll figure it out." Blake gave my shoulders a squeeze and stood.

I grabbed his hand to stop him. "Thanks for rescuing me, Blake. I'm sorry you had to find me." I stared at my fingers wrapped around his. I pulled away as warmth infused my body and ran up my neck.

"There's no reason for you to apologize." Blake crouched in front of me and took my hand in his again. "I'm sorry. We were worried." He paused. "*I* was worried. Get some sleep. Things will look better tomorrow. We'll go to Monkey Mountain."

"That sounds like fun." I grimaced. "Except the mountain part."

Blake studied me. It reminded me of my father's overprotective concern and that left a sour taste in my mouth. Finally, he squeezed my shoulder and went to his room.

I turned off the light, rolled over in my bed and let myself sob. Gunshots echoed right outside the window. I jumped and huddled under my blankets. Red and blue lights lit up the sky, and I realized they must be fireworks to celebrate the Chinese New Year.

Then I heard Emma. "Alia? Are you okay?" My bed shifted as she sat down, then she began to rub my back. I took comfort from her touch and miraculously drifted off to sleep amid the din of explosions.

Chapter 18

I was running. The stalker was right behind me. His smug smile told me he was confident he would catch me. I opened my mouth to scream, but nothing came out. I tried again and again, but something pushed the scream backward, making me gag. I bolted upright and smacked my head on the bed above me.

Emma peered over the edge. "What's wrong?"

"Just a nightmare. Sorry, I woke you." I gingerly rubbed at a tender spot near my hairline.

I lay back down.

No matter how many times I told myself it was just a dream, I couldn't get the image of the stalker out of my subconscious. My head pounded, making me feel slightly nauseous. I checked my watch. It was only five-thirty.

I didn't want to go back to sleep with the images of the haunting dream. I got up, planning on calling Craig once I found somewhere I could talk to him.

I rolled out of bed and showered. After applying a little makeup, I decided to let my hair air-dry before attempting to do something with it. I smiled at the small freedom of wearing very little makeup. I didn't know if I could go all the way to not doing my hair at all. My mom would really roll in her grave.

Half an hour later, I made my way down the stairs with my phone in hand. I stepped off the front steps and stood where I would see anyone coming and where I would be able to quickly run back inside.

I dialed Craig's number.

"Hi, Alia." Craig's voice was surprisingly soothing. Here was one person who knew all the details of what was happening.

"Someone tried to kidnap me last night."

"Are you okay? Did you call the local police?"

"Not yet, but I will this morning."

"So, what happened?"

"A fellow teacher happened to be close by and saw him take off with me."

"You were alone?"

I felt like a kid who had been caught breaking the rules. "Yeah. What happened to Agent Collins? I was with Anthony, but then suddenly he was gone, and I was lost."

Craig took a deep breath, then another. I wasn't sure if he was angry with me or the situation. "Agent Collins said he lost you when you ran off with your friend. The roads were too crowded for him to move easily."

"Earlier at the fort where we were sightseeing, I saw someone I recognized from my father's funeral."

"Do you know his name?"

I sighed. "No."

"A name would really help us out, or a picture." He paused for a moment. "I'll see if I can figure out who your person is. Do you think you could describe him?"

"I can do better than that," I said as an idea popped into my head. "I'll draw a picture of him."

"Really?" Craig sounded skeptical. " How many times have you seen him?"

"Two. But I can do it," I said with more confidence than I felt.

"Okay. Keep me updated. I'll try to find out if there is more than one person who might be after you or if that guy is the one delivering the notes."

"Thanks."

I ended the call and took a deep breath.

The door to the hostel opened. I jumped, and Blake stepped out.

"Can I join you?"

I put my hand on my chest to calm my racing heart. "I was actually about to come back in. I don't want to be out here alone."

"No kidding." He stepped off the stairs and put his arm around my shoulders.

I reached up to push my hair behind my ears. I froze as my fingers felt the damp lock. Of course, Blake was the first person to see me without my hair done. My eyes flitted to Blake then back to the asphalt.

"If you're worried about your hair," he said, as if reading my mind, "it looks beautiful."

I snorted, feeling slightly embarrassed at his praise. "I haven't done it yet."

"That doesn't mean it isn't beautiful." He gazed at me. I studied my hands, avoiding his eyes. He gently cupped my chin and turned my face toward him. Warmth shot from his hands and sent a shiver down my back. "It doesn't have to be perfect to be beautiful."

Silence fell between us as I struggled to find something to say.

He stepped back, clearing his throat. "I called the police and reported the incident. They said to call as soon as you see the guy again."

"Thanks. I hope I don't see him..." I trailed off and sighed. That was a ridiculous hope. The facts pointed to the great probability I would see him before I even left Kaohsiung. "How did he follow me here?"

"I don't know." He shook his head. "I think my heart stopped when I saw you weren't in your room. I was sure you had been kidnapped right from under my nose."

"I'm sorry. I couldn't sleep."

He sighed, "But last night you seemed as afraid of me as the guy taking you away." He stared at me intently. "Why?"

"I panicked. I'm not afraid of you. You have been my greatest confidant since I came here."

My mind wandered to the night before. The note confirmed my father's accident wasn't one, but why tell me that? Why deliver the notes at all? The first one told me the person knew I had a lot of money I had moved...at least that is what I assumed it was talking about. There wasn't anything else I had someone would want. The second confirmed what I already knew. But had my father been killed to get the money, or because he had gotten too close to exposing

Frank for embezzling? If they killed for the money, they wouldn't hesitate to kill me, except I was the only one who could get to it. What would happen if something happened? Did Luke have a secret code to the safe in case something happened to me? I trusted him implicitly, but did Frank know that? Was sending someone after me about the money, or were they afraid I had the evidence my father would have turned over to the FBI?

Ice gripped my chest. Either way, the stalker was intent on kidnapping me. If he wanted me dead, he probably would have already done it.

"Alia,?"

Blake's voice drew me out of my spiraling thoughts. "What?"

"Are you okay?"

I shook my head to clear it. "Um, yeah. Fine."

Blake took my hand. "Alia. You can trust me."

"I'm just scared. I don't think this guy will stop until he has kidnapped me."

Blake grabbed my hand. "Why would they follow you all the way to Taiwan?"

I took a deep breath. "My father was about to uncover the evidence needed to convict someone of embezzling." Could I tell him names? I wasn't sure if any of this was classified information. "He was killed. I was sure I was safe here. I'm not sure if they think I have information that could convict them or if they are only after my father's money."

Blake tightened his hold on my hand. "If someone followed you here, we better keep track of you. You don't seem to have problems at work."

I shook my head. "I've seen someone outside of the school. Though I couldn't confirm it, I felt like he was watching me."

"What?" Blake placed both of his hands on my shoulders. "Alia. You need to tell me any time you see something strange."

The door opened again, and Emma and Anthony stepped out.

"I was wondering where you guys went," Emma winked at me.

"Can I get my sketch pad before we go?"

"Do you have a bag to carry it in?" Blake asked.

"No, I can carry it in my hands."

"I brought a backpack for hiking. I'll carry it for you." Blake held the door open for me.

"Thanks." Then I latched on to what he had said. He had said hiking. Were we really going to hike? Couldn't we, just once, see a mountain without hiking it?

Blake and I went up to the rooms. He met me by the door of the girl's room and motioned for me to put my sketch pad and charcoal inside.

After getting off the bus and walking for a bit, we turned at a point where the sidewalk branched off up to the base of the mountain. There were three little pedestals, each with a statue of a monkey on it.

A little farther up the sidewalk, Blake read a sign and said, "It's a good thing we don't have food or anything with us. I imagine water is okay, but the monkeys would try to take the food if you had it. We don't want the trip marred with a monkey attack."

I jerked my head. "A monkey attack?"

"We'll be fine," Blake said.

I managed to swallow my fear and followed Blake and Emma toward the mountain.

When we got to a fork in the trail, Blake started up the path on the right. A sign a few feet later announced the monkeys on the mountain were the Taiwan Macaque. As we stepped onto a boardwalk, I saw them everywhere. They were chatting in the trees and walking on the wooden path. A little farther, one sat on a bench. Emma gave Blake her camera. "Take a picture of me next to the monkey," she said and sat down, leaving some space between her and the monkey, then she motioned for me to join her.

"No, thank you," I said. What if the monkey could smell what I had for breakfast?

"Come on, you'll be okay."

I shook my head emphatically, then Anthony leaned into me, "You can do it." He gave me a little nudge toward the bench.

Why do they care if I sit next to the stupid monkey? Finally, knowing Emma wouldn't give it up, I walked in a half circle to stay as far away from the monkey as possible. I sat stiffly next to Emma, nearly sitting on her lap. Cameras clicked as Emma smiled and I eyed the monkey warily.

I got up slowly from the bench and pranced away from the monkey back to Anthony and Blake. I wanted desperately to run but didn't want to startle the monkey so it would attack.

We climbed wooden stairs. *Why does everywhere we go involve climbing stairs?* I put my head down, concentrating on moving one foot in front of the other. I was stronger than when we hiked the Big Buddha. I had ridden my bike to school and walked to the grocery store. After a few minutes of hiking, I wasn't breathing as hard as expected.

After a few minutes, Anthony touched my back to get my attention. "Look, Alia. There are monkeys coming toward us."

Five monkeys were making their way past Emma. Anthony stepped away from me to give them room to go past us.

I jumped to the side when Anthony moved, following his lead. I landed on the edge of the stair and lost my balance. Blake caught me.

"Careful. They won't hurt you, Alia. You don't have food."

The monkeys climbed down the stairs in a line and passed right by us.

"They are close enough I could touch them!" Emma exclaimed. I hoped she wouldn't try. I savored the minute's rest as we watched the monkeys pass.

Small hands clawed at my back, and I screamed.

Chapter 19

I twisted, and a long furry tail disappeared behind me. I stumbled forward in a vain attempt to get away from the monkey clutching my clothes. Blake caught me and yanked the monkey off my back. He unceremoniously tossed the monkey into the foliage surrounding the wooden path. His hand tightened on my arm as I took another step forward to get farther away from the spot, terrified the monkey would try again. I jerked my arm, trying to wrench it free, but Blake held tight. His hand tugged at the hem of my shirt. His grip slackened, and I quickly pulled away and whirled toward him. He held up what looked like a cracker. It seemed the monkey had taken half of it with him. He tossed it in the general area he had thrown the monkey.

He stepped toward me, his hand outstretched, compassion in his gaze. A sob escaped my lips, and I flung myself into his arms. Blake staggered slightly before he caught his balance. Both his arms wound tightly around me. My body shook as I let myself cry. After a moment, my tears subsided, and Blake stepped out of my arms and held me at arm's length, studying me.

"Are you okay?"

I shook my head. "Was that cracker attached to me?"

"It was in the belt loop of your jeans."

"But..." I jerked my head around as if the answer to my unspoken question was in the trees.

Emma looked frozen in shock, and Anthony seemed sincerely sorry for me.

"Do you remember feeling something that would give us a clue as to where it came from?" Blake asked. "On the bus maybe?"

"You think someone planted the cracker on me?" That seemed a roundabout way to kill me. I had no doubt the stranger stalking me must have something to do with it.

"Well, crackers don't just climb onto people," Anthony said, making me relax marginally, but then he sobered. "Maybe it would be better for you to go home. You seem to be in a lot of danger here."

"No. I have you guys. I'll be fine. Plus, I really don't know if I would be safer in Changhua."

Blake walked a circle around me, his eyes scanning from head to foot. Shivers ran up my spine, and heat crept up my neck.

"I don't see anything else. You should be good."

My hands still shook with shock. Blake's arms around me had been so comforting, I wanted to run back into them, but I didn't dare. I was sure his feelings for me went beyond just friendship, since I never saw him holding Emma's hand, but I didn't want to push him away with my neediness.

Soon, I could only hear my heavy breathing mixed with the beautiful sounds of nature and the steady throbbing in my head. We had been hiking for an hour, but I didn't want to admit the monkey attack had affected me so much. This hike was much farther than the Big Buddha hike had been, and my out-of-shapeness was more evident than ever. The breeze rustled the leaves and the monkeys above us in the trees chatted endlessly.

"Can we rest for a minute?" I stopped and took in the beautiful deep green of the trees and plants. The trees twisted up next to the path and branched out over the boardwalk, creating a canopy, making me feel isolated from the city. It gave the feeling of deep serenity.

I sighed, willing myself to enjoy the peace. Here in Taiwan, I hadn't felt one with nature very often. I reveled in the feeling now, even though it was punctuated with the pounding in my head. Was the headache from stress or from dehydration? I didn't know.

"Here. Drink this." Anthony handed me a small bottle of Gatorade. "It might help."

"Thanks." I downed its contents at the same time I remembered Blake also had water bottles. I probably wouldn't die of dehydration, even though sweat trickled down the side of my face and pooled on the inside of my elbows. The breeze helped cool the areas. I lifted my head to bask in the delicious feeling as the oppressive and uncharacteristic February heat nearly suffocated me.

A few minutes later, we reached a map that told us we were almost to Lookout Platform where Blake suggested we go. Sudden wooziness forced me to sit and put my head in my hands.

"I can't believe I'm so weak," I cried. "What's wrong with me?"

Blake moved down the stairs and touched my elbow. "Nothing is wrong with you. It's hot."

"Maybe she needs to drink a little more," Emma said.

"No, thanks." The thought of drinking anything suddenly made me want to puke.

"Are you sure?" Blake asked.

"Yeah. I'll be fine," I lied. I was sure I was going to die. My head pounded and nausea pushed on my throat. It took all of my willpower to keep my half-digested breakfast where it belonged.

"I can't get over the fact that I'm walking with monkeys," Emma said in an obvious attempt to distract me. "They walk right past me. It's still blowing my mind."

Anthony laughed. "Yeah, the hostel hostess was telling me monkeys sometimes even go as far as the 7-Eleven we saw on the corner at the bus stop. They have even gone inside and taken things."

I snorted. "Thievin' monkeys. Think they own the place." My vision blurred and everything around me distorted making it seem like I had four knees instead of two.

"At least you still have your humor," Anthony said, standing and offering me his hand.

I managed to grab his hand so he could help me up without letting him know I had decided the middle hand was probably the one to grab. I looked ahead and saw two Blakes and two Emmas. My breakfast came closer to my mouth, so I focused on the stairs and breathing and not crying. The three inches on the map was obviously a lot farther than I would have thought. When we made it to Lookout Platform, I flopped onto the first bench I saw.

I breathed deeply to slow my rapidly thudding heart. I studied the view the platform gave of the city. The pollution in the air dimmed the city buildings, making it seem like we were viewing it through a light fog. I focused on the city as everything near me swayed to the left; the smoggy view of the city didn't churn my stomach so much.

Blake sat down next to me. "Are you okay?"

I managed a nod. I just wanted to be alone for a moment. I had to get my body under control, or I was going to pass out.

I focused on not looking like my head was spinning. My peripheral vision became fuzzy, and nausea swept through my throat and clogged there. I tried to swallow but couldn't even manage that.

Blake gave me a side hug. "You did well." He stood up and walked to the railing. His movements were so natural, so fluid. I admired his tall, muscular build as he leaned over the railing. Then the world around me, not just my head, spun. My face burned and sweat broke out around my hairline.

Anthony watched me for a moment. "You okay?" He joined me on the bench.

I forced my head to bob up and down slightly as a hard wave of nausea brought my stomach closer to my mouth. I leaned over and rested my head between my legs. Anthony's hand lightly rubbed on my back.

Suddenly, Emma's face was in front of mine. Her face kind of blurred as blackness framed my field of vision.

"Lie down for a minute, Alia," Emma ordered. She helped me lie down on the bench. I closed my eyes and put my clammy hands on my forehead. I took deep breaths, wanting my body to cooperate, so I would stop attracting all this attention.

Then a calming blackness enfolded me.

"Alia."

Someone shook my shoulder. I opened my eyes and scrunched my nose at the putrid smell of vomit.

Emma used a Kleenex to clean my mouth, but she didn't seem to notice my eyes blink rapidly.

"Maybe she's reacting from her monkey attack," Anthony suggested.

"I think it's more than stress from that," Blake countered. "She went through worse last night."

"She's just overheated," Emma said.

I nodded. Yeah, that must be it. Moving my head made a mini earthquake between my temples.

"She's waking up." Emma sounded relieved.

Waking up? I hadn't fallen asleep, had I?

"Alia." Blake touched my shoulder, leaning over me. "Can you drink a little?"

I shook my head, my brain rattling between my ears.

"Please try." His voice sounded anguished.

I swallowed hard. "Okay."

I kept my hands on my forehead. Blake helped raise my head, his hand supporting it. I took the water bottle from him and forced down a couple of sips but couldn't stomach any more. Blake lowered me carefully to the bench. His fingers caught on a tangle in my hair.

I groaned. "I didn't do my hair."

Emma raised her eyebrows. "You're dying on a bench, and you're thinking about your hair? You look fine."

A short barking laugh escaped my laboring lungs. "How can you say that now?"

She shrugged. "True. Your hair is the only thing that looks fine. Can you try to sit up for a minute?"

The nausea had eased a little and my vision wasn't blurry anymore, though my head still pounded.

"I'll try."

Blake grabbed my hand and helped me into a sitting position, scooting me farther down. That's when I noticed the vomit on the ground next to the bench.

"Please don't tell me I threw up," I groaned.

"I won't tell you." Blake supported me as my head lolled to one side.

I gripped the front edge of the bench and concentrated on taking slow deep breaths. When had I felt something was off?

I glanced at Anthony. No, he wouldn't hurt me. He was my friend. I must have drunk too much. I shook my head but stopped when it made me feel nauseous again.

"I'm sorry I'm ruining your guys' vacation," I said, filling my lungs slowly again and again, wishing I didn't feel so sick.

Blake shushed me softly, probably thinking that talking took too much energy. But existing took too much energy right now.

"Don't worry about it." Emma kneeled in front of me.

Anthony sat next to me. "You're not ruining anything."

"How're we going to get you off the mountain?" Blake asked, most likely voicing everyone's concern.

"You can leave me here," I said pathetically, "with the monkeys."

"Not on your life," he retorted. "I'll carry you if I have to. Can you try standing?"

Everything took so much effort. I clasped Blake's offered hand, and Anthony supported me by grasping my other arm. My whole body shook. *What is going on?*

Blake swept my feet out from under me.

"You can't carry me all the way down," I objected.

"We can try piggyback if that's what you prefer," he told me. "But you're in no shape to walk off this mountain."

I knew he was right. "Let's try piggyback. That might be easier for you."

"I'll carry her," Anthony offered. "That way, you can run down and get someone to call an ambulance."

"I can handle it," Blake said firmly. "I'm not leaving her."

Blake gently set me down and held onto me with one arm. He took his phone out of his pocket. "I have service. I'll call an ambulance and have them meet us."

I had a strange sensation I was floating as Blake made the call. Anthony pulled me closer to him so I could lean on him for support. Though I wasn't sure my feet were actually on the ground.

Fears of being left alone in the hospital and no way to communicate had black dots dancing in front of me again. I knew something was wrong, and going to the hospital was necessary. I vowed I would not let Blake send me alone.

Chapter 20

Once Blake had stowed away his phone, he handed Emma his backpack. Anthony gave me a boost onto Blake's back and we headed down the stairs.

I closed my eyes and used my arms to support my weight the best I could. Each step Blake took jostled my head, which increased the pounding intensity. Whether or not it was physically possible, I was sure my head would explode from the blood pounding through my veins.

"Put me down," I said as my stomach heaved. I pushed from Blake before he let go, but Anthony helped steady me and I fell to my hands and knees and wretched into the foliage. I rested my forehead on my forearms, my head swimming again.

Blake wrapped an arm around my waist and hoisted me up.

I threw up several more times; each time felt like my stomach was turning inside out. Soon, I was only dry heaving, my insides wanting to exit my body.

We were at the bench where we had taken the picture with the monkey when some paramedics charged up the boardwalk with a gurney. Blake set me down, never fully letting go of me, and helped me lie on the gurney. I clung to Blake's hand.

"Don't let me go alone," I croaked.

Blake turned to Anthony and Emma. "You can find your way back?"

Anthony grabbed my leg. "You'll be okay, Alia."

I gave him a thumbs up in response, hoping I looked brave.

I regretted having to ride the gurney as it bounced over the boardwalk. My grip tightened on Blake's hand, and I squeezed my eyes shut against the pain.

"Hold on, Alia. We're almost off this. Then it will be smoother." Blake's words came out labored as he jogged next to the rapidly moving gurney.

It wasn't until we were in the cooler interior of the ambulance that I realized the front of my shirt stuck to me with sweat. Blake's shirt was also soaked. "I'm sorry," I whispered, but couldn't manage more as the paramedics put an oxygen mask on me.

After being poked and prodded, the nurse finally left me alone with Blake. Doctors thought I had been poisoned, but I had thrown up enough that there wasn't lasting damage. I thought it was food poisoning since we had eaten breakfast at a street vendor, and I had always been a little leery of the cleanliness of those places.

"I'm sorry, Alia," Blake said.

"It's not your fault."

Blake leaned against the chair he had pulled next to my hospital bed and ran a hand through his hair.

"How long do they think I need to stay?" I asked.

"They want to keep you overnight."

I grimaced. At least Blake was here now. I already dreaded when he would leave for the night, and I would have to try to communicate with the nurses.

"Can you think of anything someone gave you?" Blake asked.

"You think I was poisoned on purpose?" I hadn't seen anything suspicious. "I didn't take anything from a stranger, unless it was where we ate breakfast."

Blake scrunched his eyes together, and then made a phone call. "Anthony?"

"She was poisoned. Do you know if that drink you gave her was ever out of your sight?"

I held my breath as I waited for Blake to speak again.

"It's okay, Anthony. You didn't know. She'll be fine... No, she doesn't hate you."

I gestured for the phone. Instead of handing it to me, he put it on speaker.

"Anthony, I don't hate you, and I don't blame you." From what I had heard, there may have been a lag of time when Anthony had left the drink unattended.

"I'm really sorry, Alia."

"All is forgiven. It was an accident."

"Thanks, Alia." Anthony sounded so depressed I wanted to reach through the phone to give him a hug.

"So?" I asked when Blake had hung up.

"He said the drink he gave you was in his room the whole time we were gone to Cijin Island."

"Then Anthony is lucky he didn't drink it."

"I don't know if I would say it was lucky, since you ended up in the hospital."

"I guess not," I said. "But I'm willing to be the sacrifice in this instance. It all worked out."

"I'd rather you not be a sacrifice at all." He leaned over me, gently brushing his lips against my forehead. "Get some rest." He grabbed my hand again, stroking each knuckle with his thumb.

How could I sleep? He had just kissed me, and he was holding my hand in a way that sent sparks shooting through my fingertips. Not to mention someone was probably also after Anthony, since his drink had been poisoned.

I closed my eyes as Blake pressed his lips to my fingers, sending more shockwaves up my arm.

When I woke next, it was dark outside my window. My chest tightened as I searched the dim room. A soft snore made me catch my breath. Blake's head was resting next to my waist. He hadn't left me. He was asleep. I let myself run my fingers through his hair. It was soft and thick. I twirled that curl that always brought my attention to his brilliant blue eyes. I twirled it around and around my finger, letting it slip enough that I never actually touched Blake. And in that moment, I realized—if I was reading him correctly—this was more than a little crush. Why didn't we speak of our feelings more?

My heart ached with the desire for him to hold me, to kiss me. My cheeks warmed at the thought. My dad wouldn't have appreciated me coming home from Taiwan in love. He might have even thought I was being impulsive, but it felt right.

Blake stirred, so I retracted my hand.

"Alia?" he whispered.

"I'm awake, but it's late. Why are you still here?"

"You want me to leave?" His confusion was evident.

"No." I hurried to reassure him. "I'm glad you're here, but I don't want you to be uncomfortable."

"I'm fine. I didn't want to leave you here alone." He paused. "I mean. You can't communicate with probably most people checking on you."

"What time is it?" I asked.

Blake checked his phone. "Just after three."

I didn't know what came over me, but with the darkness, I felt less vulnerable. "Blake?"

"Yeah."

I took a deep breath, squeezed his hand. "Do you feel it, too?"

I prayed he understood what I was talking about, and I wouldn't have to be more forward. But since the moment I first touched him, the connection was palpable.

"You mean this?" Blake kissed my fingers. He shifted in the darkness, his silhouette hovering over me. "And this?" His lips brushed my forehead and fire flowed from his lips and spread through my whole body.

"Yeah," I whispered.

"I feel it. And wish I could act on it. But I can't."

"Why not?"

"You're in danger right now. If the people who are after you know about your feelings for me, they may try to use me as some kind of leverage. I don't want to put you through that."

"You're right." I sighed. "I would feel awful if anything happened to you."

Blake's hand cupped my cheek, and his thumb gently caressed my lips. "You better get more rest. We both need to sleep." His lips lightly brushed my forehead again. He was right. I did need to sleep, and I knew I would have sweet dreams the rest of the night.

Chapter 21

The next afternoon Blake helped me climb the stairs of the hostel, and after I brushed my teeth three times to get the gross aftertaste of sickness out of my mouth, I got settled in bed.

"Those mints I gave you didn't do the trick, huh?" Blake joked.

"They helped but didn't clean my teeth."

I was feeling a lot better but I wouldn't be doing a lot of physical activity for the rest of the day.

After Emma asked me for the tenth time what she could do for me, I knew I wouldn't get any rest if she stayed in the hostel, so I insisted she go sightseeing with Anthony. Apparently, Blake was not willing to leave me alone, but Emma said he was in his room. I wished he would come in and talk to me, but it was probably better. I would want him to kiss me. But I couldn't risk having anyone see and use him as leverage.

I fell in and out of a wonderful dreamless sleep. When I was awake, I didn't allow myself to think about being poisoned or almost kidnapped. I relived that intimate moment with Blake in the hospital over and over, savoring the warmth that flooded my body when I thought about it.

My sketch pad was sitting on top of my bag. I remembered I had told Craig I would sketch the guy from the cemetery, who was now following me around Taiwan. I propped myself up and got to work. I shuddered as I focused on making his black eyes just right. I had to erase his nose and try several times before it looked correct, but when I was done, I felt I had a pretty good likeness of him. Tired out from the effort, I let myself sleep, hoping the face on the paper wouldn't appear in my dreams.

My phone ringing startled me awake. It was Craig. I hurried to answer the call, my hands fumbling slightly.

"Hello?"

"Alia. Are you okay? My FBI agent said you might have been poisoned."

Where was Agent Collins hiding? I tried to think how they would know I had been poisoned, but I gave up. I was sure they had their ways.

"I'm okay. Just resting today. I hope to get out of bed tomorrow."

"Do you know who it might have been?"

"I can't think of anyone. I think it was probably food poisoning. Unless the stalker guy knows where I am staying. My friend, Blake, thinks it might have been a drink Anthony gave me. Blake called Anthony, and he admitted the drink had been left unattended yesterday."

"They don't know the full extent of your case, do they?"

"Blake knows quite a bit," I admitted.

"Alia. You've seen a picture of Frank Barlow, right?" Craig went on before I could answer. "I want you to watch out for him and call if you even think you see him."

My stomach jumped even at the thought. I hoped I never ran into him. "You think he's here?"

"We don't know for sure. We are still checking flights. Just continue to be safe. Stay with others. We'll figure this out."

"Okay. I drew a picture of the guy stalking me. I'll send it to you. Hopefully, that will help."

"Sounds good."

I ended the call and sent Craig a copy of the drawing.

Seconds later, my phone dinged, and Frank Barlow stared back at me from my phone. It was a picture of him at a party. My dad was standing next to him. My heart lurched, then it stopped altogether when I caught sight of a blond-headed guy slightly behind him. It was the same stranger who had been following me. I sent off a text, telling Craig he was also in that picture. Maybe having a real picture instead of my drawing would help.

My stomach jumped to my throat when there was a knock on the open door. It was Blake.

"Hey, stranger," I said, faking nonchalance.

Blake held up a to-go box. "I brought you some dinner."

My stomach clenched at even the thought of food, but I knew I needed to eat to get some strength back. "What is it?"

"Some fruit." He strode forward and helped me sit awkwardly on my bottom bunk.

After a few bites, I felt my appetite returning. I sighed.

"What was that sigh for?" Blake asked.

"I think I may live after all."

"I think so too." Blake chuckled at my joke.

"I thought I had lost all traces of humor when my father died," I admitted.

"Then maybe you are finding some healing."

Tears unexpectedly sprang to my eyes. "I still miss him...and my mom."

Blake wrapped both arms around me. "I wasn't saying you didn't. Healing and forgetting are two different things."

My arms were pinned to my side, holding my dinner, but I wanted to drop the food and melt into Blake. I was safe and secure with him, and I liked the feeling. The security I had with my parents was different. It was hard to put into words, but the only thing I could come up with was I thought Blake understood me even more than my parents had. I had hidden a part of me to conform to what they expected.

The week break from teaching was dragging on with all that had happened. I wanted to return to Changhua, but didn't want to put anyone out. I knew Emma had looked forward to this trip.

The next morning, we made our way to a bus station, and after a two-hour ride—where I mostly slept against Blake's shoulder—we entered a town where the streets were lined with shops showcasing swimming suits, flip-flops, sandals, sundresses, shorts, and tank tops. One main street ran the length of the town, making it seem quaint.

"Are you sure you're up to this?" Blake asked as he nudged me awake.

"Yeah." I needed some air.

We wandered in and out of shops on our way to the beach.

"I think I might buy a swimsuit," I said. The water looked nice.

"You think you can swim?" Emma eyed me doubtfully.

"Maybe just wade. I'll see."

"Then let's buy you a swimsuit." Emma steered me into a store. "You guys wait here." She waved her hand to shoo the boys out of the storefront. Blake took up a militaristic stance in front of the store with his feet spread apart, facing the street, his hands clasped behind his back.

We found a cute dark pink one-piece swimsuit. It had large blue flowers printed on it and matched my skin tone exactly. It was perfect. I felt like a little girl playing dress-up as I showed it off to Emma. I left the swimsuit on and paid for it.

The lady behind the counter grinned. "Very beautiful."

I thanked her in Chinese and met the boys outside. Blake's eyes nearly popped out of his head, and Anthony's mouth dropped open.

I gave them a little shove to move down the street. "If you guys stare at me like that, I'm going to change back into these." I held up my bundle of clothes.

Both guys blushed and focused on the road in front of them. We came to a place where we walked down some wooden stairs past the fence that hid the beach from view. People were crowding the beach at the entrance, so we made our way through until we found a place that wasn't overly crowded. Blake pulled out the beach towels from his pack. I laid mine next to Blake's, feeling an inexplicable need to be near him. I piled clothes at the top. Then I sat down and hugged my knees, resting my chin on them, staring out into the ocean.

Anthony sat next to me. "Are you going to swim?"

"I'll rest for a minute."

Anthony and Blake both took off their shirts and ran to the water. Blake's muscles moved in a rhythmic motion. My jaw dropped open and then I shook my head. I was acting like the boys had when they saw me in my swimsuit.

Blake slid out of the waves and stared at me, his lips quirking. My eyes were locked on him, almost like I was entranced. Rivulets of water ran down his naturally tanned skin and over his well-toned muscles. He looked away and I grinned.

"What're you smiling about?" Emma asked.

"Nothing." The sun warmed my skin, almost uncomfortably. "Do you think Blake packed any sunscreen?"

"I don't know." She turned to the ocean and yelled, "Hey, Blake! Do you have any sunscreen?!"

"It's in my bag!" He yelled back.

Emma gave him a thumbs up and retrieved the bottle as Blake and Anthony walked up.

"I better put some on." Anthony dried himself, applied sunscreen, and headed back to the water. Emma followed suit.

Blake got some sunscreen and then handed me the bottle. I applied it to my face, legs, and arms. Blake settled on his towel, his arms resting on his knees. He studied me with an odd expression.

"What?" I asked.

"I was thinking about that note." He looked to the ground. "We were with you the whole day. I can't remember seeing anyone suspicious."

"I know. And the cracker in my pants?"

Blake nodded. His brow furrowed toward Anthony and Emma for a moment. He opened his mouth, then shut it and shook his head.

"Is someone just trying to scare me? The note said my father's death wasn't an accident. Could they be after me, too?" I wiped an errant tear, determined not to cry anymore.

"Ali..." He paused.

My eyebrows shot up. "What did you call me?"

"Ali. I'm sorry, it just slipped out."

"It's okay. It's...It was my father's pet name for me." I laughed lightly. "My mom hated it. She loved my name and wanted him to use it, but he loved calling me his 'little Ali'." I laughed lightly at the memory. "You can call me Ali... if you want."

His lips turned upward slightly before a frown settled. "Ali, I'm so sorry for your loss. I can't imagine how hard that is."

I tightened my grip around my legs. "I feel so lost. I don't know what I'll do when I go back home. My neighbor, Grace, is my closest friend. But she's seventy years old." I rested my face on my knees as I let my eyelids close. The sun warmed my arms, but the light breeze carrying the spray from the ocean cooled me.

I sensed him scoot closer and energy pulsed around me. He slipped his arm along my arm and tugged my hand free, before bringing it to his lips. I opened an eye and lifted the corners of my lips up to show him I was okay. He squeezed my hand and whispered into my ear, "I can think of at least three people who are your friends, Ali. And we think you're amazing. I can't speak for the others, but I will do all I can to help you figure out who is after you."

My smile turned more genuine. His bright blue eyes contrasted brightly against his tanned skin and black hair. They were intense and searching.

"Thanks." I leaned my head against his shoulder as he let go of my hand and wrapped his arm around my waist, pulling me close.

"Ali..." His eyes grew serious, intent on my attention before he continued. "You bring such joy to the kids, playing games, teaching, talking with them. When you draw, there's an ease to your fingertips, but a tension line between your browns that, I admit, is adorable. You give yourself so little credit, but I've seen your strength. I *admire* that strength. I might be even a little envious of it." He raised his hand, brushing a strand of hair that had escaped my ponytail, his fingers barely brushing my cheek. I was surprised I heard his next words over the pounding of my heart. "Ali... I am in complete awe of you."

I pulled away a fraction and stared at him with my mouth slack for a moment. Then his lips were caressing mine before he pulled back quickly and his eyes darted around. My breath caught as the sensation of his lips on mine lingered.

"Sorry." He grinned. "I forgot about all the people. I can't risk having the wrong people see us." He stood and held out his hand. "Are you ready to get in the water?"

The sun was no longer the only thing warming my face as I let him help me up. I was invigorated by his touch and his light kiss that made me want more, but left me breathless. I gazed out over the ocean where the waves lapped the shore. Beyond the beach, cliffs came together to form a cove. The water sparkled in the sun. "It looks wonderful."

He put his arm around me and pulled me close, his lips brushing against my ear. "I'm glad you're doing better." His breath tickled, and I couldn't help the giggle. Energy continued to course through my body. The allure of his touch, his light kiss...Everything made me want to stay by his side.

The cold, refreshing water seemed to soak up my fatigue and wash it away with the waves. I stopped when the water reached my knees, needing a moment to acclimate to the cold.

Blake ran into the surf, diving in when it reached his waist. Emma swam leisurely on her back. Anthony stood after getting knocked into the water by a big wave. I laughed, feeling liberated.

Anthony joined me. "Are you feeling okay?"

"Yeah. I think I might even try swimming a little."

Anthony gave me a squeeze. "You're beautiful, you know?"

I met his eyes. He smiled, but there was something in his eyes I couldn't explain. Sorrow maybe?

"Thanks."

Anthony stepped away, diving into the water again.

I glanced back, debating on how much I should push myself. My body froze, despite the heat of the sun. The guy from the cemetery stood not far from our stuff. I turned to find Blake, but when I couldn't spot him immediately, I turned back to the guy. He had disappeared into the crowd. I frantically searched the beach, my heart rate increasing. That was my chance to show Blake who it was.

A hand touched my back, and I screeched and turned to see Blake. "Oh, Blake," I breathed. "You scared me."

"And you're scaring me." He studied me. "You're not going to pass out, are you?"

My throat closed as I fought panic. I ignored his question but told him the truth in a strangled whisper. "I saw him, Blake. He was there, then he wasn't." I pointed to where I had seen the stranger.

Blake's hand became firm on my back and pulled me into him. I buried my face in his neck, hiding my face from the world that seemed intent on making me crazy with fear. Blake put his other arm around me and tightened his grip. "It's okay, Alia," he murmured. "I won't let anything happen to you."

"How can you promise that?"

He met my gaze. His eyes serious. "I'll do my best."

My hands rested on Blake's chest, and his muscles twitched under my touch. With each twitch, my breath hitched slightly. I closed my eyes to shut out the fear and uncertainty, thoughts of my father, his death, and that someone was trying to harm or kidnap me. It was all too much. I couldn't take it anymore. I wished I could dig myself a hole to hide in until the FBI caught Frank.

I sat in the cold water. The surf surged forward, reaching my chest. I scooted backward until the water was only covering my knees when it lapped in. I supported my weight with my arms and closed my eyes, knowing Blake was watching and wouldn't let anything happen to me.

The constant flow of water over my legs slowly relaxed me. Fear was replaced by determination. I had grown so much in the last month, and it wouldn't have happened if I hadn't come to Taiwan. I wouldn't let the stranger rob me of my newfound independence. I would fight.

I stood, waded out to my waist, and with a last look at Blake to be sure he was still nearby, dove into the cold water. I swam several feet beyond where I could touch, enjoying the freedom. Then it struck me.

This was how Dad died.

Chapter 22

Two hands pulled me under the water. I kicked and turned to see who had me, but the water stung my eyes. My knee connected with what I hoped was my attacker's face, and I fought to the surface for a breath before I was dragged back under.

I fought his grip as my lungs struggled for air.

One strong arm wrapped around my waist and yanked me from my attacker. I gasped for breath as my head broke the surface.

"Are you okay?" Blake asked, searching my face.

I sucked in air and searched the water, sure my attacker would reach for me again.

Blake dove into the water and resurfaced a moment later. "I can't find him. There are too many people. How does he disappear so easily?"

Blake propelled me toward the shore. My breaths came in gasps and a sob escaped.

Blake helped me get to the towels. I fell onto my towel and lay on my side, letting myself cry.

I heard him speaking Chinese and knew he was calling the police.

"They'll be here in a minute," he whispered.

I sat up. "Thank you. You saved me again."

Blake swallowed several times and held the phone away from his mouth. "I couldn't live with myself if something happened to you."

Emma and Anthony sat next to me before I had a chance to respond.

"Are you okay?" Anthony asked.

"What happened?" Emma asked at the same time.

I gave them a short version of what happened since I knew I would have to repeat it when the police arrived. Emma's eyes were wide with fright, and she wrapped her arms around me. Anthony patted my knee and told me how sorry he was.

Soon, sirens rang through the air, and Blake was explaining what happened. Police officers spread out across the beach. One guy asked me some questions, but Blake answered for me without translating. I was grateful. I didn't want to think about it.

It seemed forever before the police left with translated statements from me, Emma, and Anthony. I sighed in relief.

"Can we head home?" I asked.

"Of course." Emma gathered up our things while Blake helped me to my feet. I didn't think Emma really understood what I had meant. I wanted to go home to Idaho, but I couldn't until the FBI said so. I held my clothes as we made our way to the bus stop. Emma and Anthony fell asleep within a few minutes of boarding. After a few moments of silence, I turned to Blake. Needing a distraction.

"What're you thinking?" I asked.

"You first."

I looked out the window at the houses, fields, and snatches of ocean passing by my window. "I want to go home." I tear slid down my cheek and I brushed it away. "I wish I could rewind the past three months, but if I did that I wouldn't meet you. And my students…" My throat constricted, and I had to clear it. "My students have made me feel needed."

"You can go home if you want, but I'm not sure it will be much safer."

"You're probably right."

"What were you thinking?"

"That I wish I could protect you better. I am glad I have been able to meet you. You're not what I expected."

"What were you expecting?"

"Not the warm-hearted person I know you to be."

I laughed. "Was I that cold on the airplane?"

"You were quiet, but you were also grieving, so it makes sense." He nodded toward my bundle of clothes sitting on my lap. "Do you want to put those in my bag?"

"Sure." I moved the pile to him. White caught my eye and I put my hand on his arm to stop him from stuffing the clothes in the bag. I didn't want him to see my bra, so I stuffed the white down, only to realize it was paper. My heart pounded in my ears and my muscles refused to move.

"What?" Blake's attention went to my hands, so I fished the paper out of my shirt. All my attention riveted on a white slip of paper.

I held it for a moment, my hands shaking. I didn't want to know what it said. Had the stranger put it there?

Blake stuffed the clothes into the bag. There was no envelope this time.

"Blake?" I whispered. "This stalker could have easily put the paper on my clothes."

"You may be right."

Relief swept through me, which was ironic since the stranger had tried to kill me. I was so glad there was only one person here tormenting me.

Blake nodded toward the paper in my hand. "What does that one say?"

My fingers shook as I opened the fold in the small slip of paper.

You would have been safer if you stayed at home.

I dropped the note. Blake picked it up and scanned it. He studied me for a minute.

"Blake..." I cut myself off. My mind whirled. Yes, my life had been threatened here, and yes, I wanted to go home, but what would have happened if I had been home when some guy kept showing up at my house claiming he had to do repairs? It might have been easier for him to kidnap me.

Blake set the note on his lap and pulled me close to him.

"It's not true," I mumbled into his chest. "Someone's also been showing up at my house. Grace was knocked out because she threatened to call the police to his face."

"Shhh. I know, Ali."

I pushed away from him. "How do you know?"

"I'm just saying I believe you."

Emma gasped. She leaned over the aisle, reading the note. Blake snatched the note and stuffed it in his pocket.

"What're we going to do tomorrow?" I asked Emma, trying to distract her.

"Are you sure you want to go out again?" Emma replied. "You've had it pretty rough the last few times. Almost kidnappings, poisonings, and now attempted drownings haven't smothered your vacation fire?"

"The alternative being to lie around by myself at the hostel?" I asked.

Emma shrugged, an apology in her eyes. "How about you make a suggestion for something you want to do," she said.

"Maybe we should spend the rest of our vacation at home," Blake suggested. "It would be safer since we can lock up our apartments. Plus, the change in plan might throw your stalker off."

I agreed and I would rather sit around at home than in a hostel we were sharing with strangers, but I hated to end the trip early for Emma and Anthony.

"Maybe you and I could head home," I said to Blake. "And Anthony and Emma could stay and finish out their vacation."

Emma looked torn. I could tell she wanted to do more sightseeing, but she also felt bad for wanting to have fun when I was getting into all this trouble.

"It's okay, Emma," I said before she could argue. I longed for some alone time with Blake. "You can stay."

Emma stared at me a moment longer, the debate evident in her eyes. "Okay. You might benefit from having the apartment all to yourself. Just don't answer the door until you confirm it's Blake."

"Deal." I would only be alone at night if I knew Blake. I needed a few days to know it was safe at my apartment.

Chapter 23

I studied my students as they finished writing in their communication books. Being back in their presence brought me joy. I was needed here.

My throat closed slightly, and I had to clear it. "Okay. It's break time."

The children cheered.

"Teacher," Steven said as he came up to my desk after I sat down. "You miss us?"

I laughed. "Yes, Steven. I did miss you."

"I miss you, but not speaking English."

"Oh?"

Steven grinned and shook his head.

Emily came up behind Steven. "You should have come to Taipei."

"I'm sure that was a lot of fun. But I went to Kaohsiung with the other teachers."

"You go to Kenting?" she asked.

"Did you go to Kenting?" I repeated, using the correct wording. "Yes, I did."

"Kenting is fun. I like swimming." Emily wandered to her desk, leaving me with Steven again.

"You swim in Kenting?" he asked.

"Did you swim in Kenting?" I chuckled slightly as he rolled his eyes. "Yes, I did." I shivered as I remembered the stranger dragging me into the ocean.

Steven went to play a game with some of the other boys. After a few moments to myself, my three musketeers, as I liked to call them, Emily, Ivy, and Elaine, crowded around my desk.

"You happy to see us?" Emily asked.

"Yes, I am very happy to see you. Are you happy to see me?" I asked, modeling the proper way to speak.

Emily shrugged but smiled.

"Oh, yes," Elaine said. "You my favorite teacher ever."

"I'm your favorite teacher you've had here?" I clarified.

Elaine nodded vigorously. "I like you best."

"Me, too," Ivy said. "You very nice."

"You are too sweet."

Break ended, and I picked up the book I was reading to them. My heart nearly burst. I had never felt such intense love for anyone other than my parents.

I hoped being home meant the guy would give up tormenting me. I thought I could relax better here, which was ironic since I had returned from a vacation.

Saturday, I sat in my apartment alone while everyone else had home visits. I had locked the door right after Emma had left. I did not like being completely isolated. My one solace was the fact that somewhere, some FBI agents were keeping an eye out for me. Plus, there were security guards in the lobby. I paced around the apartment, trying to figure out what I should do, until slumping onto the couch and shutting my eyes tight.

I retrieved my sketch pad, desperate to distract myself. Emily's face came into being as a rough sketch on the page in front of me. She was tomboyish. She would play the rougher games with the boys, and once when I took them to the park to play kickball, I saw her athletic skill and competitive streak up close. Ivy was quiet and reserved, but willing to speak her mind. I blinked away tears as I sketched her shoulder-length hair and brown eyes. I really had missed them. Elaine's picture was last. She, too, was shy, but was the first to offer help when I needed it. She didn't raise her hand to answer questions, though. I drew each of their faces in small proportions so all three would fit on one page.

I studied the rough sketch critically. Something wasn't right. Their sweet personalities were not evident. Erasing some of the rough lines caused by my chaotic thoughts, I tried again. The lines continued to be rigid. I closed my eyes and took a deep breath. If I wanted to remember these sweet girls forever, I needed to get this right. My facial muscles slowly relaxed as I breathed deeply and willed my mind to focus only on the love I felt for these sweet girls. I put my pencil to the page, and my heart swelled as I remembered them surrounding my desk during their break this week. I loved my younger art students, but these girls were different. I felt a connection to them. Their quirky personalities delighted me.

Memories of taking little drawings to the old folks' home flashed into my mind. They always showered me with praise. They would smile and pat my hand with their wrinkled and blue-veined hands. In the aftermath of first my mother's, then my father's death, I had forgotten my love of making people happy with my art.

Ivy, Emily, and Elaine reminded me of that love. They had helped replace a dark depression with a glimmer of hope. Now their sweet faces were captured on the page for me to remember. These girls would always hold a special place in my heart. Looking at their picture soothed my soul, and I almost forgot I was alone.

A knock on the door startled me. My heart hammered in my chest. Blake and Anthony were also gone. The only people I would welcome the sight of would be the FBI agents.

I put my drawing down on the couch beside me, my breathing erratic as I stared at the door. The doorknob didn't jiggle as though someone was attempting to open the door. I counted silently to ten before I dried my hands on my pants and eased toward the door. Whoever was there didn't knock again. Maybe they assumed I wasn't home. I had my thumb ready to call Craig if someone was on the other side of the door.

I cracked open the door to peer through. A white envelope floated to the ground. I scanned the hallway and didn't see anyone. A flare of anger coursed through my veins. I ran into the hallway letting the door bang behind me. I passed the elevator to the stairs, hoping to catch the person red-handed.

Adrenaline pushed my body past what I thought was possible for me. A door exiting the building at the bottom of the stairs closed. I followed, and the door shut behind me. I found myself in a narrow alley between the apartment complex and the building next to it. Pausing to catch my breath, I realized the stupidity of my actions. What did I think I was going to do if I caught him? I turned back to the door, but it was locked. Frustrated, I hurried to the back of the building where I could enter those doors. The door behind me banged open. My heart jumped to my throat, and I sprinted away. Somehow, I had gotten in front of the stalker. I glanced behind me, but no one was there. He exited the doors at the back as I turned the corner. I screamed and ran toward food street, hoping I could beat him there, not knowing where Agent Collins was at the moment. Who knew where the other agent was.

His feet pounded behind me. He was going to catch me. I couldn't run any faster.

"Stop!" The voice sounded far away, but there was no way I was going to listen.

The steps behind me faltered, and I surged ahead as hope bloomed inside me.

My heavy breathing tore at my chest as I skidded around the corner. A booth near the corner wasn't open yet, so it was empty except for the equipment needed to cook their food. I ducked under the equipment and squeezed my way to the back.

My breath caught in my throat, and I concentrated on taking slower breaths, waiting for the stalker to pass. I peered through the space under the fryer and soon legs came into view, but I didn't dare move to see his face. He cursed.

I waited for him to move forward. My legs cramped, but there was no way I was going to sit on the filthy ground.

"I lost her... I saw a guy matching the picture she drew leave the apartment...He's gone...It's just me today...I'm not sure how he got into the apartment complex without me seeing, but I saw him leaving so I followed... Then I realized he was chasing her... I called for him to stop... Apparently, my presence made him change his mind about chasing her, but I don't know where Alia went."

I was pretty sure it was the FBI agent. I moved so I could see over the equipment I was hiding behind.

His eyes widened. "Never mind. I found her."

He hung up.

"It's okay, Alia. It's me. Agent Daniel Collins."

"I know." My heart continued to pound. I crawled out of my hiding place, and Agent Collins offered me a hand up.

My phone rang. It was Craig. I took a deep breath before I answered, sure I was going to get an earful.

"Alia, what were you thinking running?"

"Sorry." I was tempted to explain, but I knew I would be babbling. It was stupid of me to leave my apartment.

"Now that I've officially met Daniel, can I meet the other agent?" I asked.

"I prefer to keep him anonymous, just in case there is someone else besides the stalker after you."

I wished he wouldn't sound so cryptic. "Okay. Thanks." I ended the call and shook Agent Collins' hand.

"Nice to finally meet you, Agent Collins."

"Just call me Daniel. Come on. Let's get you to your apartment before your stalker sees me with you. I'll have to find a hat or something to change up my look."

"Right. Sorry."

"What made you run after him anyway?" Agent Collins asked.

"I got another note." I shook my head, still appalled at my impulsiveness. "I guess I lost my head."

"Do you have it on you?"

I felt my pockets. "No, I think it's lying on the floor near my apartment."

When we got to my apartment, I found the envelope inside my apartment. With hands trembling, I ripped it open and extracted the small piece of paper. *I am always watching you.* Well, I knew that. Did the guy think I was stupid?

"Can I take it?" Agent Collins asked.

These notes would be used for evidence.

"Hold on, and I'll grab the others I have." I was back out of my bedroom a moment later, and I handed them to Agent Collins, grateful to be rid of them.

"Don't overreact next time, and lock the door." Agent Collins shut the door behind him.

I turned the deadbolt.

What was I thinking? *Did you already forget what happened in Kaohsiung, Alia? You could have been kidnapped or worse.*

Determination flared inside of me. I wouldn't let him mess with my mind. I would figure out who this person was. I retrieved my phone.

Me: Luke, do you know many of the people who worked for Frank Barlow who would also know my dad?

It was a long shot. I had no idea if my dad had given him any details, but I was determined to try.

Luke: Anyone in particular?

Me: Someone with blonde shaggy hair who is about my age.

Luke: No. Sorry. What's up?

Me: I am wondering if the guy who is stalking me/trying to kidnap me works for Frank for sure. It would help the FBI.

My phone rang. I sighed. I should've known better than to say that last bit.

"He tried to kidnap you?" Luke asked—well shouted—with no preamble.

"Yes, but it was while we were on vacation. My friend saved me. It was only because I got separated from the others. I'm perfectly safe here." I think.

"Maybe you need to come home."

I wanted to go home, but only because it held the illusion of being safe. The note at Kenting had said I would be safer at home, but since it was the stalker who delivered the note, I doubted he was telling the truth.

"But you said a man had come to my house a few times posing as different people and even knocked out Grace."

"He hasn't been back for three weeks. He must have figured out you weren't home and now he's obviously trying to get you kidnapped. Frank is determined."

"I know I'm in danger, but I would be completely alone at home."

"I'm sure the FBI would still be watching."

"Yes, but I would be a prisoner in my own home. I'll stay with someone at all times from now on."

"If something else happens, you better be on the next flight."

"Okay." I prayed it wouldn't come to that. Here, I had Blake to watch out for me as well as the FBI. At home, it would only be the FBI. I would feel completely isolated.

Chapter 24

"Hey," Anthony said after class was over. "Will you be my Valentine?" He wiggled his eyebrows, which made me laugh.

I almost said yes, because I felt bad saying no. My stomach clenched and a foreboding crept up my back. I couldn't shake it.

"How many valentines is one allowed to have?" I asked, trying for a teasing tone. He hadn't actually asked me on a date. Maybe that would have been his follow-up question.

"You already have a Valentine?"

"Well, no," I admitted. "But I was…well…" Heat shot through my cheeks.

"You would rather have Blake be your Valentine?"

My face burned hotter, which I didn't think was possible. "Maybe?"

Anthony patted me on the back. "No problem. No need to be so embarrassed."

I forced a laugh and watched Anthony saunter out of the room.

Blake was waiting for me in the teacher's lounge.

"Can I take you out to dinner?" Blake asked. His neck reddened. But for that little clue, I would have never guessed he was uncomfortable as he leaned casually against the desk.

"I'd love that."

"That's good, 'cause I already have reservations," Blake said.

"Reservations?" I asked. "That sounds fancy."

"Only the best for you," Blake said. "Are you okay to go now, or do we need to stop by the apartment building?"

I held up my very large purse-like bag.

"We'll go drop that off. Then I think we may just take a taxi." He put a hand to my back and let me lead the way home.

For the umpteenth time, I thought about mentioning my latest note to Blake, but I didn't want to ruin any potential this night had. Besides, Agent Collins knew about it. That was who needed that information. Plus, the note hadn't scared me; the way it was delivered did, and I didn't want to admit I had run after the guy. I could see Blake chastising me for that.

Fifteen minutes later, we climbed into a cab and Blake told the driver where we were going. Then he slid his fingers through mine and pulled me closer. My heart fluttered at his touch, and I wished we could show this affection in public. I didn't know how this date wouldn't alert the stalker, but I wasn't going to argue.

When we exited the taxi, I glanced around. The shops on the street sold scarves, shoes, clothes, and hats. Any food we would get among these shops wouldn't come from a fancy place Blake had described.

"So, where're we eating?"

"Tasty's." Blake pointed to a building not five yards away, sporting a large red sign with the restaurant's name.

Blake put a hand on my back to steer me in the right direction, but dread slid down my spine. I scanned the crowd around us but didn't see anything alarming. I shook myself. Blake's eyes flicked to the spot I had studied then returned to my face.

"What is it?" Blake asked.

"I think I'm getting jumpier." I hated to admit, even to myself, the last note had gotten to me. At least I was being cautious.

Blake pressed his lips into a thin line and raised an eyebrow. I knew he didn't believe me, but he must have thought it best not to press me.

We entered the restaurant, and Blake spoke to the gentleman who showed us to a table.

After we ordered our food, Blake leaned back in his chair with his arms folded. I thought he would ask me about my behavior in the street, but he smiled.

"Anthony said he asked you to be his valentine first."

I ducked my head and organized the silverware. At least I wouldn't have to blunder through the meal using chopsticks. Blake's hand covered mine.

"Don't worry. He wasn't offended. I think he knows how we feel about each other. Emma has mentioned she knows." He chuckled as I raised my eyes to meet his. "I guess we haven't hidden it very well."

"Is that going to be a problem?"

"With me?"

"With the stalker. Maybe even with Sara."

"As long as we stay professional at work, I don't think Sara will even notice. I don't know about the stalker. It will probably be best to keep things casual for a while longer."

"But you asked me on a date."

"I couldn't resist." He lifted my hand and kissed my fingers over the table.

I squeezed his hand as he released mine and a warm tingling sensation crept up my arm and into my chest. Our meal came, and the conversation ceased for a moment. He couldn't resist taking me on a date. The thought alone was enough to send my heart racing.

I was halfway through my meal when the hairs on my neck prickled. Trying to appear relaxed, I arched my back in a show of stretching and turned my head slightly. I inhaled so quickly I almost choked on the bite I was still chewing. In a far corner, the man stood staring at me. In fact, he was smirking. His lips curled, and his eyes shifted from me to Blake. Blake stood. The stranger's eyes flitted to Blake, then he moved deeper into the shadows to another exit.

"Is that him?" he asked.

I nodded. I forgot Blake hadn't seen him clearly before.

Blake rushed after him. I waited, my eyes glued to that exit. I didn't dare follow. Here in this crowded restaurant, I was safer than I would be in the dark alleys.

Soon I heard the familiar wail of police sirens. I put my head in my hands and rested my elbows on the table. Would this ever end?

"Ali?" Blake's words next to my ear made me jump.

I shook my head. There was no use lying. The stalker knew we were on a date. He could use Blake as leverage.

"Come on. Let's go talk to the police at the entrance, so we don't bring too much attention to ourselves."

I allowed Blake to help me stand. He said something to the waitress, then led me to the entrance where we met the police.

Blake talked to them for a moment in Chinese. Then turned to me.

"Can you describe him? I'll translate."

Instead of answering, I pulled up the sketch I had sent to Craig. "Is this close enough?"

Blake's eyes widened. "When did you draw that?"

I shrugged. I couldn't tell him I had drawn it for the FBI.

"It's a good likeness."

I handed him my phone and Blake talked to the man again. I rested my hand on Blake's arm to get his attention. "He also has blonde shaggy hair and dark eyes."

Blake nodded and spoke some more to the policeman.

"Can I send this picture to him?"

I nodded and Blake fiddled with my phone then returned it before retrieving his phone. Curious, I leaned over his arm to see that he had sent the picture to himself and was now typing numbers into his phone as the policeman spoke.

"You sent it to you first?" I asked when the policeman had left, and we had returned to our table.

"I wanted the policeman to have my number instead of yours."

"Thanks." I shook my head. "He invades my apartment, and now interrupts my date," I mumbled. Then realizing I said them out loud and stuffed food into my mouth, hoping Blake hadn't heard.

"Invaded your apartment? When? Did he hurt you?"

"No, he just delivered a note...to my door."

"Ali. Why didn't you say something?"

"I didn't want to let it bother me. The note itself seemed so ridiculous."

"What did it say?" Blake asked.

"I am always watching you."

"No wonder you're jumpy. When did you get that one?" Blake's insistence to get answers was flattering, but also a bit annoying. I had it under control. FBI agents were helping me.

"Last weekend."

Blake touched the back of my hand. "Please don't keep any more notes secret."

"I won't," I promised. I had already told him about the other notes, and Craig had said that was okay.

A week later, the secretary, Lucy, found me right before my level 1 class started.

"Alia. Your fan is ready. Come." She beckoned me, flapping her hand with her palm down.

My heart skipped a beat. I grabbed my purse from the teachers' lounge before going to the front door where the gentleman who sold fans was waiting.

He handed me a thin rectangular box.

"Open it," Lucy said.

I opened the box, carefully extracted the fan, and unfolded it. My breath caught in my throat and tears threatened. Beautifully depicted on the thin but stiff paper were the pictures I had drawn.

Memories of my parents.

"Oh, it's beautiful." Tears pricked at my eyes. I blinked them away, not wanting to cry, but I missed my parents so much.

"It felt right to paint your beautiful picture on the fan for you," the man said.

I paid the man, thanked him in Chinese, folded and returned the fan to the box.

I ran up the stairs and found Blake in his classroom. I had to show him. We still had ten minutes before class started. Most of the kids were still making a ruckus downstairs.

I held up the box, unable to speak.

"He brought your fan?"

I held it out to him.

He opened it, and his eyes widened. "It's breathtaking, Ali." He looked at me. "I watched you draw it for him but couldn't see the picture."

Tears formed despite my efforts to keep them at bay.

"Oh, Ali." Blake carefully folded the fan before pulling me close.

My heart ached. I couldn't breathe. Grief rose in my chest, closing my throat so I couldn't even speak. Blake held me, stroking my hair and murmuring between kisses on my head. Footsteps sounded up the stairs, so I reluctantly pulled away.

Blake wiped at the tears on my cheeks. "It's okay to miss them. I'm always here if you need someone."

"Thanks, Blake. I better go put this away before class begins."

I rushed past the students stampeding up the stairs and headed to the teachers' lounge. Anthony was there. I didn't want him to see my tears, so I lowered my head and set the box in my bag before rushing.

There were still tears in my eyes as I entered my classroom.

"Teacher, you okay?" Elaine asked.

I wiped at the tears. "Yes, I'm fine." I started class while thinking about how Blake had been the one to insist I order a fan. I was so grateful he did.

Chapter 25

Blake showed up the next morning to walk with me to church. He was strangely quiet.

"Blake? Are you mad at me?"

He startled, like he had forgotten I was there. He took my hand.

"Sorry, Ali. No. I'm not mad at you. I'm just worried. That guy saw us on the date on Tuesday. I'm sure he put two and two together. He knows we have some feelings for each other."

"I haven't seen him since then." I didn't believe that meant we had seen the end of him, but I wanted to give Blake some comfort.

"Ali..." Blake's voice cracked, which tore at my heart. "I couldn't live with myself if anything happened to you."

"You can't protect me forever." *As much as I wish you could.* But I didn't want to be that vulnerable with him yet.

Blake opened his mouth, but then closed it and nodded once. I kissed him on the cheek.

When we got back from church, I hugged Blake before turning to my apartment.

"Wait." Blake's arm scooped me behind him. "Is Emma home?"

Baffled at his behavior, I shrugged.

He pointed to the floor. I couldn't see anything alarming.

"Let me check your apartment first."

"Okay..." He opened the door slowly. An envelope had been slipped under the door. I was impressed Blake had seen it. Blake disappeared to the bedrooms.

I picked it up at the same time Blake appeared through the entryway that led to the hall.

"Emma is gone." The panic in his voice caused me to clench the envelope.

I immediately called Emma.

"Hello?"

"Emma, are you okay?"

"Yeah?" She sounded confused.

I breathed a sigh of relief. "Good. Sorry to bother you. Another note was delivered to the apartment, and I got worried when you weren't home."

"What?" Emma's voice was a little shrill. "I'm sorry. I'm in Taichung. Stay with Blake until I get home."

"Okay." I wouldn't fight that. I ended the call and opened the envelope.

Not everyone is who they seem to be.

The next day, I couldn't get the note out of my head. Who was not what they seemed? My first thought was Agent Collins, since I didn't know him well, but Craig had sent me a picture of him. The only other people I was close to were Emma, Blake, and Anthony. The thought that any of them held secrets related to this mystery made me sick to my stomach, so I ignored any thoughts about them. I would go crazy if I was suspicious of everyone I knew.

Friday night, I stood in the kitchen, wondering if I should cook something for dinner or go to food street, when someone knocked on the door.

It was Anthony.

"Hey, Alia! Do you want to come with me for dinner?"

I smiled away a knot forming in my stomach, though I couldn't identify the reason. "I was just thinking of going to food street. I'm glad to have someone to go with."

The elevator had just opened when Blake came jogging up to us.

"Mind if I join you?"

Anthony raised his eyebrows at me.

"The more the merrier," I said, grateful it wouldn't feel like a date, since I didn't want to lead Anthony on. Blake stepped inside the elevator with us. The prick of unease immediately disappeared. It must be because I felt so comfortable around Blake.

Anthony hardly talked through dinner. I had hoped he had invited me as friends, but his attitude said he might have been hoping it was a date. It was probably better Blake had invited himself as a third wheel. I wanted to be in a relationship with Blake, but we had to pretend our feelings for each other were platonic, though both Anthony and Emma knew otherwise.

When we got back, I stopped Anthony as Blake went into their apartment.

"Anthony. Are you okay?"

"Yeah," Anthony assured me. "It's for the best."

I scrunched my forehead in confusion. "What was for the best?"

"Nothing. Thanks for coming with me, Alia. You're a beautiful person."

"Thanks, Anthony. You're a good man."

Anthony's lips formed a thin line.

"Really. Anthony. I'm so glad we get to team teach a class together. I love working with you."

"Thanks."

Then he turned and disappeared into his apartment, leaving me wondering if he was mad at me.

The next morning, I was sitting in my apartment, deciding what I wanted to do. I hadn't seen the stranger lurking in shadows, and I hadn't received any more notes, but it had only been a week.

Emma was gone on a home visit, but I hadn't asked Anthony or Blake what their plans were. I was too busy trying to figure out Anthony.

It was almost ten o'clock in the morning when I jumped at the sound of someone knocking on the door. Adrenaline shot through my veins as I crept toward the door. I cracked the door open slowly, peeking through the crack.

It was Blake, so I flung it open and nearly threw myself into his arms, I was so relieved it wasn't the stalker or another note. Instead, I gave him a little wave.

"Hey."

"Hey. Did I scare you?"

"I'm a little jumpy after last week."

Blake's lips tightened. "What're you up to?"

"Nothing much yet," I said, willing myself to act as comfortable as Blake was, even if I didn't feel it. My heartbeat an irregular rhythm as I took in Blake's oh-so-attractive dark, slightly curly hair. He had dressed up more than usual with a polo shirt and jeans. My eyes drifted from his face to his arms and chest, then to his bright eyes. "Did Anthony have a home visit, too?"

"Yeah. Do you wanna wander around town with me?"

"Yes," I said. "I can't stay cooped up in the house all day. I should have asked you last night if you had a home visit."

"I had some things to do this morning, and I wasn't sure how long it would take."

I wondered what things he had to do but let him lead the way to our bikes. We drove up and down roads, stopping to wander down a street full of vendors. Blake eventually stopped in front of an open gate with a sign with "Confucius Temple" written on it. We didn't say much as we wandered to the temple. The red roof practically glowed in the bright sunlight. The heat was sweltering, and it was only the end of February. We entered through white doors. Peace enveloped me, which was a sharp contrast to my rolling thoughts throughout the week as I had failed to figure out who the note had been referring to. I had almost convinced myself they had said that just to make me edgy. Almost.

The inside was cooler, but still muggy. The familiar smell of incense burning infiltrated my senses. I didn't think I would ever get used to the smell. I followed Blake's lead and took off my shoes at the entrance. We stood in silence as we examined the tall ornate containers on what looked like some kind of altar. The two outside containers held flowers. The others appeared empty. Plaques inlaid in gold and silver lined the back wall. I didn't dare ask Blake to translate. I didn't want to disturb the reverence that pervaded the small building. The hot humid air outside cleared my head as we exited and found some benches. Blake sat down and patted the spot next to him.

It was clear he wanted to talk to me but wasn't sure what to say or how to say it. My hands went clammy. I rubbed them on my pants and played with the hem of my shirt, wishing I didn't feel so uncomfortable.

"Ali," Blake started, then shook his head. "I'm sorry I interrupted your date with Anthony last night."

I touched his hand, and he stopped.

"I'm glad you came. Anthony's disappointment proved he had asked me on a date when I thought he was inviting me as friends. I only want to date you." I paused. "You are the only person I feel free to be myself with, and with that last note... I'm so confused."

"Ali. I care a lot about you. I know I told you we couldn't be seen together, but I want us to be a couple, to date and see where the relationship can take us." He took my hand and brought it to his lips.

The many warnings my father had given me about men and how I couldn't trust any of them sprang to my mind. I cringed. *Great time to think about that, Alia.*

Blake studied me. "What?"

"My thoughts are just running away with me. My father always scared every guy who came near me. He thought guys would only like me for my looks." I paused. "And wouldn't see the real me."

His eyes opened wide. "You are beautiful. But I'm attracted to who you are."

My lips twitched a little, but I sighed. "Sometimes I'm not really sure who I am, but I'm trying to find out. It's been an experience to get to know me so far away from anyone from my former life. No one even knows I'm here. Coming here was the bravest thing I have ever done."

Blake's eyebrows rose. "No one knows you're here?"

"Well," I amended. "I guess that isn't true. A few people know."

"I want you to find out who you are. I'll try my best not to be in your way. Can you find who you are and also date me?"

I thought over the last two months since I had come to Taiwan. I did know who I was. Teaching and being with the kids brought out the best in me. I felt at ease when I was with Blake. I was rediscovering my hopes and dreams, the dreams I had let take a backseat to what my dad thought I should do. I had never verbalized what I truly wanted in my life. My parents' wishes for me became my wants, no questions asked.

Blake was patiently watching me, a small smile on his face, like he knew the conclusion I was coming to.

I met his gaze. "I do know who I am. I want to use my art to lighten someone's day, to touch them. I want to teach that love to others."

"And you are doing that here," Blake said. "I love that. I want to see more of it."

My chest expanded so much I felt like I might burst. It was too early to say it out loud, but I thought I might love this man.

Chapter 26

It was almost dark as I made my way from food street after getting dinner later that night. I had seen Agent Collins trailing me discreetly, giving me the confidence I needed to find some dinner alone. I was walking on air. Blake wanted to take our relationship to the next level. I still wasn't sure what that would entail and what would happen when we went home. We hadn't talked about that, but I was content to enjoy my time here.

A strange moaning drifted on the warm breeze. Everything inside me stopped. I didn't dare move, but I forced my eyes to search the area. I didn't know where Agent Collins was. The last I had seen him was buying something at the vendor next to where I got dinner. Had the stalker attacked him? My panic turned productive as I searched the grounds near the apartment complex door. A pair of legs sticking out from behind a bush caught my eye, and I rushed forward.

I pulled my cell phone out of my pocket and had Blake's number ready to push call. I considered calling Agent Collins' number, but I wasn't sure those legs didn't belong to him. Plus, I needed Blake to help me call an ambulance. I had my thumb on the call button as I rounded the bush. The person was lying face down on the cement.

It was Anthony. After searching the area one more time, I carefully turned him over. The sound of a gasp made me jump before I realized it was me. Anthony had been beaten, badly. He was moaning but didn't appear to be conscious.

I dialed Blake.

"Hey, Ali."

"Blake," I whispered. "I need your help."

"What's wrong?"

I could hear the urgency in his voice.

"Come out to the bike rack. We need to call an ambulance." I hung up before he could respond.

"Alia?" The sound of Anthony's voice brought my attention to his prostrate form.

"It's okay, Anthony," I soothed. "Blake's coming and we'll call an ambulance." I looked around for Agent Collins. He seemed to materialize behind a building. I waved him forward.

"Listen to me, Alia." Anthony reached for me.

"Just lie still. We'll get you help."

Anthony shook his head. "I deserve to die."

"What, no. What are you talking about?"

Anthony laughed, but it sounded bitter. "Alia, I've been a fake." He grimaced.

I stared at him. His words weren't making sense. Is that why he had been distant the night before?

"I've been planting the notes."

I sat back, the bushes scratching my arms. Anthony? My friend who I had been teaching with, who could make me laugh? He was the one delivering the notes?

Tears leaked out of the corner of his eyes as he squeezed his eyes closed. Time seemed to slow. I continued to grapple with what he said. A part of me wanted to reject what he said, while the other part of me wanted to get as far away from him as possible. How? Why? My tongue was heavy. I couldn't yell. I couldn't scream. All I could do was stare dumbly as I watched tears flow down his cheeks. His eyes begged for something I didn't think I could give. He delivered the notes. That meant he had been working with the stalker this whole time.

"Alia!"

"Over here, Blake." My voice sounded strained, so I stood so he could see me.

"What's wrong? You gave me a..." He stopped when he caught sight of Anthony.

"Call an ambulance."

"What happened?" Blake asked as he put the phone next to his ear.

"I don't know. I found him like this."

"Alia?" Anthony's voice was barely audible.

I kneeled down next to him. My desire for answers overrode my desire to stay away.

"I..." He swallowed hard. "I also planted the cracker at Monkey Mountain, made sure you got separated when we got off the ferry from Cijin Island, and gave you the poisoned drink. Frank told us to scare you into going home yourself or kidnap you." He gasped and took a few breaths. "I couldn't bring myself to kidnap you myself, but I tried to help Bridger."

I sat back. I couldn't speak. I wanted to run. But Anthony went on.

Anthony closed his eyes. "I deserve this. Uncle Frank sent me here four months before you came. He knew you had signed up somehow. He wanted me to get comfortable, so you would trust me. Uncle Frank wanted to be prepared in case he had to kill your father. But he knew if he killed him, we would probably have to silence you as well, since he didn't know how much you knew. When you first arrived, I was supposed to keep an eye on you, so Frank could work to access your funds, but when he failed and couldn't get inside your house, he changed tactics. We couldn't seem to get you alone, and the few times we did, Blake came to the rescue." He opened his eyes but wouldn't meet my gaze. "I was supposed to pretend to like you, but you never wanted to go anywhere with me." He arched his back slightly and grimaced. "I let Bridger know where you were going."

He paused for so long I thought he had passed out. "Anthony?" I reached out to touch his shoulder to see if he was still alive. But when he spoke again, I yanked my hand back. "Last night, I was supposed to ask you out so he could kidnap you. When Blake came along, Bridger was furious. He wanted me to try again tonight. I couldn't do it. You told me I was a good man. I knew I wasn't, but it meant so much that you thought so. I didn't want to hurt you, anymore."

He smiled, but it looked more like a grimace. "I told Bridger I was done helping him. He beat me and left me for dead." He took a ragged breath.

Blake was speaking Chinese into his phone, so I knew help was on the way.

"Does he only want my money?" I asked.

"It started that way." He paused again. "But Uncle Frank thinks you know too much now. You won't be safe at home."

Anthony coughed, and I was mortified to see blood. I backed away. Cold dread infused my body despite the warm night air.

The ambulance arrived, and Blake and I got a taxi and followed it. I sent a quick text to Emma to let her know what was happening. Blake held my hand as we sat in silence in the waiting room while my heart seemed to sink into an abyss. I had trusted Anthony. He had been pretending the whole time. He hadn't really been my friend.

It wasn't long before the doctor came out and talked to Blake.

Blake turned to me when the doctor left, his face hard. "He didn't make it."

I slumped to the floor, and my body shook with wracking sobs.

"What did he tell you?" Blake asked, after a while.

I knew Emma would want to know what happened. "I'll tell you now if you'll tell Emma."

Blake nodded. The pain of betrayal washed over me. I took a deep breath. Blake deserved to know he had been tricked as well. Blake was his roommate and didn't have any idea what Anthony was up to. The words Anthony had said tumbled out of my mouth, as if getting it out as fast as possible would make it hurt less. But I was wrong. My chest constricted, as if saying the words made them truer.

When I finished, Blake's jaw was clenched, and his eyes were darker than I had ever seen them. He wrapped his arms around me and held me tight. My lungs struggled as the pain washed over me and I allowed myself to grieve for Anthony, or for the person I thought he was, and to grieve his betrayal. I thought it hurt when my parents died, but I knew they loved me. The pain of betrayal felt dark, and like my heart was being torn in pieces.

"Did he say who the stalker was?" Blake asked after a moment.

"His name is Bridger. He mentioned his uncle. I wonder if Bridger is Anthony's cousin." Tears still running down my face. I almost said something about him probably being Frank Barlow's son or something, but then remembered he didn't know about Frank. I made a mental note to call Craig tonight.

"Hi. Alia. I heard about your friend, Anthony. I'm sorry," Craig said before I could state my reason for calling.

I laughed despite the sharp pain in my chest. "How is it you already know why I'm calling?"

"It's my job."

"True. So, will this development help you figure out who Bridger is?"

"Frank's son," came the instant reply. "Still searching for a positive ID matching your picture to the name, but Frank does have a son named Bridger."

"Bridger killed his own cousin?" It shouldn't have surprised me. I mean, these guys were proving they would stop at nothing to get my money, short of blowing up my house, but then the passwords were inside it.

"Craig?" I prodded.

"Yes?"

"Does Frank know the passwords to my accounts are in the house?"

"I don't know, but I think he thinks the key to access the money is there since someone has tried hard to get in through means that wouldn't trip the alarm."

"Craig...Anthony said he didn't think I would be safe at home."

"We're working on a contingency if we don't catch Frank before you come home in a couple of months."

"Thanks, Craig."

"Try to get some sleep, Alia. I know it's late there."

"Thanks." Though I doubted I would get any sleep.

Chapter 27

The next day I wasn't sure I could make it through church, but I needed the peace I felt there.

Once the music started for the opening song, I started crying. I felt so many emotions, I couldn't even feel peace. Betrayal and anger warred for my top emotions, but those were quickly overshadowed by guilt for being so angry at a dead man.

"Let's skip the second hour today," Blake suggested.

"Good idea." I allowed him to lead me out of the church.

Blake turned at the pond and led me to my favorite place to sit. My eyebrows crinkled in confusion, but I shook my head. It was just a coincidence. I had never been there with him.

I sat next to him, and he put his arm around me.

"Alia. I'm sorry. Do you want to talk about it?"

"Not really. I feel angry and betrayed, but in the same breath, I feel guilty for being so mad at someone who is now dead." It really wasn't about what Anthony did. His betrayal seemed to accentuate the fact that my father had kept a big secret from me. It wasn't fair.

Blake pulled me into a hug.

"Why did he leave me in this mess?" I mumbled, more to myself.

"It's maybe a little less of a mess than if he would have gotten you alone."

I was confused for a moment before I realized he thought I was still talking about Anthony. "That's not what I was talking about. I think Anthony's betrayal brought up the similar feelings I have had since my dad died."

"Ali." Before I quite knew what was happening, he leaned down and kissed me. He broke contact a second later. I wanted to savor this moment. Forget all of my fears and anger. I cupped his cheeks and brought his lips to mine for another kiss.

Blake wrapped his arms around my waist and brought me close, deepening the kiss. His lips explored every part of mine, and I felt myself falling into him. The anger dissipated. I didn't want this moment to end. Blocking out everything around me, I concentrated on Blake's lips on mine and the hunger I felt there.

When I pulled away, I was breathless. My cheeks heated at my closeness to him.

He kissed my forehead. "What do you think could happen between us when our time here is done?"

"I try not to think about it."

"If you don't want to move away from your family home, I could get a job in Idaho Falls."

"You would do that for me?"

"I'm afraid I'm in too deep not to try to win you over completely." He kissed me softly. He took my hand before leading me to our apartments, my heart soaring with hope I didn't know was possible right now.

I had gone a whole week without seeing Bridger. I was starting to think he had given up since he had killed his accomplice—his own flesh and blood. Emma had tried to convince me to go shopping with her, but I had declined. I was home alone and enjoying the quiet. Blake and I had plans to go out again in the afternoon.

I had retrieved my sketch pad. I started sketching the sunset on Cijin Island. I had finished the rough sketch when a soft knock echoed across my apartment. Maybe Blake had decided not to wait until the afternoon. I cracked the door open to peer out and a piece of paper floated to the floor. No envelope this time.

I glanced at the note, determined to tell Blake, but Blake's name on the paper gave me pause. I shut the door quietly.

Alia. There are things you don't know about your father's company. He was involved in illegal dealings, even if he wasn't aware of them. He owes my father large sums of money, but you moved it before my father could get his share. I saw you with Blake. Yes, Anthony told me all about your little romance. If you don't want me to do to Blake what I did to Anthony, you will meet me by the pond. You know the place. I better not see someone with you. Yes, I know about your shadow.

He must mean my favorite place to sit and sketch. Agent Collins had followed me there before. That must have been why Bridger hadn't tried to kidnap me. He had known about the agent.

I forced myself to think logically. If I went to the pond, Blake would figure out I was gone and look for me. Dread slipped through my veins, making me shiver. I knew if I met Bridger, he would kidnap me. But...maybe I could work with Agent Collins and capture him. I sent a quick text to Collins.

Me: I got another note.

His number appeared on my screen. He obviously thought this was too important for a text.

"What does it say?" Agent Collins asked.

"He wants me to meet. He threatened Blake."

"You can't go."

"Agent Collins, listen to me." I took a deep breath and prayed my idea would work. "I won't go without you nearby. But if we convince Bridger I am alone, he'll act, and then you can ambush him. I know there is another agent somewhere around here. You can call him and have him in a position to help."

"I don't know, Alia. There is a lot that could go wrong. He might kill you."

"He won't kill me. They need me to get the money." Of that, I was certain.

The silence between us extended for a moment.

"Agent Collins?"

He sighed. "I think that is probably our best bet at catching him."

"Okay, I'll come down, and we can make a plan."

I quietly closed the door, not wanting Blake to follow me and get hurt.

I took the stairs down to the next floor before grabbing the elevator so Blake wouldn't hear the ding of the doors opening. I stepped into the main lobby and spotted Agent Collins waiting in the corner. He was on his phone. I assumed he was talking to his partner. He hung up before I reached him.

"Okay, Alia. Where are you supposed to meet Bridger?"

"At the pond where I've gone to sketch."

He nodded. "Okay, I'll walk a ways behind you until you turn the corner, then I'll give you ten minutes. Hopefully that will be enough time to convince Bridger you're alone."

"He might see you following me. Maybe I should pretend to lose you by running, then hiding and you run past, then find a spot to wait."

Agent Collins considered that for a moment, obviously searching for any flaws.

"Okay, I'll follow you for a block. Look back and catch me then lose me. I'll give you ten minutes from then, so get there quickly."

I took a shaky breath, willing myself to be brave. Bridger had tried to kidnap me without police back up. I could do it with their help. But my heart still beat irregularly.

Agent Collins put a hand on my shoulder. "Are you sure about this?"

"Yes." The catch in my voice gave away my fear.

Agent Collins eyed me for a moment. "Okay, let's go."

After doing my best to appear to lose Agent Collins, I rushed to the pond. The closer I got to the meeting place, the slower my steps became. Agent Collins was waiting ten minutes. If I took too long to get there, our plan wouldn't work. I forced myself to up my pace.

I slumped onto my favorite rock, then immediately jumped to my feet again. I wasn't going to go with him willingly, but I wanted to try to buy some time.

"I knew you would come. As my father told me, love makes you weak."

I whirled to face Bridger. He was only a few paces away. I took a small step back, putting more space between us.

He lunged forward, and I sidestepped. Would he chase me? I ran toward the street. Agent Collins wouldn't be that far behind.

My foot caught on a tree root, and I sprawled forward.

Bridger grabbed my arms. He rolled me over, keeping a tight grip on me. He had a length of rope in his hand and made short work of tying my wrists together.

"I figured you wouldn't come easily. Just like your father. Fighting to the last."

"What do you know about my father?" I spat, grateful for the anger rushing through me. Anger produced an urge to act, to do something. I kicked up at him. My knee connected with his jaw. He fell backward. I rolled away and fought to get to my feet. My manacled wrists made it difficult to find my balance, and I pitched forward. Bridger grabbed my leg and pulled me toward him, my face scraping against the pebbles and dirt.

He pressed his knee on my legs and wrapped a rope around my ankles.

"The more you fight, the worse it'll be for you," Bridger said.

Tears welled in my eyes, washing out some of the dirt.

Bridger groaned as he hoisted me over his shoulder before he staggered to his feet. My stomach slammed into his hard shoulder, knocking the wind out of me. My body bounced helplessly against him as he made his way through the trees.

Fear and panic consumed me, but there was no way I was going to let him carry me away. How would he explain this to any people we ran into? *Come on, Agent Collins. Anytime now.* I kicked my legs as best I could and screamed with everything I had. A hot jolt of pain exploded in my side as Bridger's fist slammed into my ribcage. I gasped as the pain spread through my side.

Something crashed through the trees behind us. Bridger turned and cursed.

Someone slammed into Bridger from another direction. I dropped to the ground and pain shot through my shoulder as I landed.

I rolled over and saw Blake struggling with Bridger. Blake wrestled Bridger onto his stomach and pinned his arms behind him.

Agent Collins ran forward, his gun drawn. Blake clapped handcuffs on Bridger. My brain felt muddled.

Bridger started laughing and turned toward me. "Isn't this a surprise? Your boyfriend even has secrets."

Agent Collins helped Blake pull Bridger to his feet.

"Tell the local PD to come get him," Agent Collins said.

Before I could figure out why Agent Collins was talking to himself, Blake pulled out his phone. "Agent Hanson here." He shook himself and switched over to Chinese.

Bridger smirked. "Even I was duped, princess. Don't take it too hard."

My thoughts spiraled out of control, but one thing stood out clear: Blake was the other FBI agent sent to watch over me.

Chapter 28

Had all of it been fake? The connection between us, the kisses? Had it all been for show, as part of his cover?

Blake hung up and ran over to me, pulling a knife from his pocket. Tears streaked down my face. Blake didn't care about me like he had insisted. He just wanted me to trust him so he could do his job.

I was his job.

Blake cut the ropes and held my face in his hands. I wanted to pull away, but I couldn't even do that. The mind-numbing pain of his deception sucked the fight out of me. No matter how good his intentions were, he had taken advantage of my feelings to make his job a bit easier.

"Ali? Are you okay?"

Blake's voice snapped me out of my misery long enough to jerk away from him.

"No."

Bridger was still laughing. "And you thought he was interested in you."

"Shut up!" Blake stood.

Agent Collins raised his hand. "Let it be."

Taiwanese men in uniforms swarmed into the area.

Bridger yelled over their rapid-fire Chinese. "You'll never be wanted for anything other than the money your father stole."

I slumped to the ground. My chest constricted, and I started to breathe shallowly. How could I have been so stupid?

When Blake returned to my side, I couldn't stop the tears. I had been such a fool.

Breathing was hard, but I had to ask. "Is it true?"

Blake came closer but stopped as I scooted away. I wouldn't let him comfort me until I heard the truth. He sighed and rubbed his hand through his shaggy hair.

"I was assigned to watch you." He kneeled and lowered his voice. "I didn't know I would lose my heart in the process."

Lose his heart? Was he still acting? I had trusted him all this time. Trusted he reciprocated my feelings for him. Now I wasn't sure.

"No wonder you tried so hard to stick by me." The words came out filled with venom.

"Ali. It was my job to stick close by, but, to be honest, some days I forgot it was my job. I wanted to be near you."

"Come on, Alia," Agent Collins interrupted. I took the hand he offered, stepping past where Blake still kneeled on the ground. "We have to get you on the next plane."

"Why? You have Bridger."

"We don't know for sure if he didn't have someone else helping him. We need to get you where we can have more agents watching you."

"Okay."

Agent Collins supported me as we started back to the apartment building. I couldn't even look at Blake without a sharp pain ripping through my chest.

Collins and Blake sat on the couch while I showered and threw my belongings into my suitcases as quickly as possible. When I appeared in the living room, Agent Collins stood. I'll go get the car and pull it up front.

"I'll come with you." I didn't want to be alone with Blake.

"You wait here with Agent Hansen." Agent Collins left without another word.

Blake reached toward me but stopped abruptly when I flinched. "Alia." Blake's voice was thick with emotion, but I concentrated on my anger and hurt. "We had been working with your father to bring down a major jewel trafficking ring, but when he went to Baja, we lost track of him and—"

"I don't want to hear about it right now, Blake."

Blake grabbed one of my bags.

I reached for it. "I can carry my own bags."

"Let me help. Please." His pleading tone broke me down a little, and I nodded.

"What about your bags?"

"They're already downstairs. I took them down while you were in the shower."

As we drove from the apartment building, I regretted not being able to say goodbye to Emma. I sent her a text explaining I had to leave right away because of a personal emergency.

I stared out the window, ignoring the ding of my phone as a couple of texts came in. My mind replayed over and over the last words Bridger had said to me. "You'll never be wanted for anything other than the money."

I knew my father hadn't stolen the money. Bridger had been trying to goad me, but the words still hurt, and part of me believed him.

My phone rang. It was Craig.

"Hello." I didn't even try to hide my despondency.

"Alia. You're on your way home?"

I chuckled without humor. "I think you know the answer to that question, but I appreciate you letting me feel like I have some control."

"It helps to make you feel like you don't have someone who knows your every move."

"I appreciate that."

"Anyway, I think it would be best if one of the agents stayed at the apartment with you. Agent Hansen said you're Mormon?"

My heart twinged. "Yes sir."

"Would it raise less suspicion if you were married or living with a man, unmarried?"

"Definitely the first." I had my standards and Grace knew them and she would never believe any other cover up story. I doubted she'd believe I would come home married, but it was our best option.

"Both of them have clearance and training for this kind of cover. You can choose the agent you are more comfortable with. I don't care which one."

I glanced at Blake in the back seat, then at Agent Collins. I didn't want to pretend I was married to anyone, but if I was honest, it would be easier with Blake. I was hurt, but that didn't change the fact that I had felt a connection with him.

"I think Bl...Agent Hansen would be the best choice for that."

Blake raised his eyebrows, so I quickly faced the road. I didn't want him reading anything into that. I didn't know if there could be a real future for us, but I needed protection.

"Hopefully, we can get Bridger Barlow to talk so we can get a clue as to where his father is."

I didn't know how to respond, so I didn't.

"Good luck."

"Thanks." I ended the call and closed my eyes.

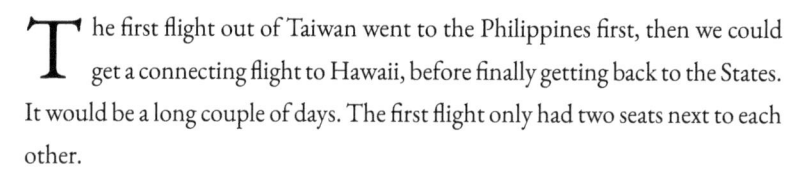

The first flight out of Taiwan went to the Philippines first, then we could get a connecting flight to Hawaii, before finally getting back to the States. It would be a long couple of days. The first flight only had two seats next to each other.

"You better sit by her." Agent Collins told Blake, taking the ticket in a seat at the back of the plane.

As soon as we were settled, I took my sketch pad out of my carry-on. I flipped through my pictures, stopping at the picture of Eileen, Emily, and Ivy. I would never see these girls again. My heart was breaking in so many ways I didn't know if I was going to survive. Tears splattered against my arm. I wiped them off and turned the page, flipping to the scene on the beach at Cijin Island. I worked on that, ignoring Blake.

I could feel Blake watching me, but I tried not to let the feeling unnerve me.

Blake broke the silence. "Are you okay?"

I studied my drawing. All the lines were jagged and sharp. The picture wasn't as good as I had drawn for the fan guy. Did Blake notice that? "Yeah." I lied. "Why?"

"Your knuckles are turning white."

I loosened my grip and took a deep breath.

"Ali. I'm really sorry. I couldn't tell you and risk blowing my cover."

I shut my eyes tight, trying to block out the pain.

"I know you don't believe me. My job required me to hang out with you, but I wanted to be near you. More and more, I wanted a close relationship with you."

"Did the kisses mean anything?" I whispered, looking out the window.

"I would have never kissed you if I didn't love you."

My eyes jerked up to meet his. "Love?" I stared at my picture in my lap, not wanting him to see the hope blooming in my chest. I didn't know what to believe anymore.

"Yes, Ali. I love you. Believe me. It was not planned. I came thinking you were going to be some spoiled rich girl who couldn't take care of herself."

I snorted. "I had no idea what kind of money my father had."

"I know that now." He shook his head. "I was even told so in my briefing, but I couldn't believe your dad could have so much money, and his daughter not know about it. Maybe that's why he was so good at infiltrating the company we were watching."

Blake put his hand over mine. "Ali. Your father was instrumental in getting us the knowledge we needed. We almost have everyone involved in jail. If we can find Frank Barlow, we will have finished what your father started."

"Did Frank kill him?"

Blake shook his head. "We aren't sure; they did a good job of making it look like an accident. Your father's last communication with us is the only clue it wasn't." He held up his hand when I opened my mouth to speak. "I'm not certain I can tell you what the communication was, especially here." He nodded at the people around us. Most of them were Taiwanese, but I supposed a good portion could understand us.

"I do have something for you." He pulled out an envelope from his carry on. My name was scrawled across the front. "I was given permission to show it to you."

"What is this?" I asked.

"I found it in Anthony's room. Sorry, you can't keep it, but I convinced Craig you could read it."

I slowly unfolded the paper inside.

Alia,

Words cannot express how sorry I am. I'm not certain you will get this, but after tonight's failed attempt to get you alone, I don't know if I will have another chance to talk to you. I can't do it. I can't continue to help Bridger. You are a beautiful person, inside and out. I wasn't expecting the drop-dead gorgeous woman who stepped out of the van that first day.

But tonight, you said I was a good man. I know it isn't true, but I love that you believe that of me, that you can see something that perhaps I can't see. Hopefully, you will be safer without me around.

Anthony.

I choked on a sob.

"I'm sorry Ali. Anthony tricked both of us."

I met Blake's gaze. "He was sorry." I forced out a breath. "But it still hurts. It all hurts."

Blake placed his hand over mine. "I'm sorry I hurt you. I hope you'll find it within you to forgive me."

I slid my hand out from under his and stared out the window and watched the clouds thicken beneath our plane. What had I been thinking suggesting Blake be the one I pretend to be married to? It was going to be like picking at the scab and keeping the wound fresh.

I clenched and relaxed my jaw several times, willing my brain to think. Blake said he loved me, but I wasn't sure I could believe him. I had thought I loved him. Maybe this would be my chance to see if we really weren't meant to be together.

Chapter 29

The universe was conspiring against me. The connecting flight to Hawaii also didn't have three seats together, so Blake and I sat alone again.

When it was clear that most of the people around us had fallen asleep, Blake turned to me. "Are you ready for this?"

I didn't want to talk about a fake marriage, but I wanted to talk about all that I was feeling. Blake had always been a good friend. I may be able to get through this if I thought of him as a friend. If I hadn't fallen for him, it probably wouldn't have hurt so badly that he had been sent to protect me.

But his kisses had felt so real.

"I'm scared," I admitted. "I'm scared to face my father's death. I'm scared Frank will find me before we can find him. How could my father keep all of this a secret and leave me to clean up the mess? It isn't fair."

"I know. It's okay to be scared. If it helps, your father could see your strength."

"My strength?" My father had never said anything about thinking I was strong.

"He knew you had it in you to finish what he started. To catch the master behind the biggest jewel embezzling operation in years. That was why your father started doing business with CORE-TECH. He knew what they were up to and went to the FBI to offer his help. He put all the money Frank paid him in a different account to use as evidence when he found out about the embezzling. Not a cent of that money belongs to Frank, despite what Bridger said."

"So what really happened in Baja?"

Blake glanced around the plane. "We'll have to talk about that later."

O nce we were in a car provided by the FBI, Agent Collins said he would meet us in a couple of days. I was left alone with Blake again.

"Okay, Alia," Blake said once we were on the freeway. "What is our story going to be? We need to be on the same page."

I had avoided talking about our fake marriage through all the flights and layovers. It was all too much.

"What do you mean, our story? We got married." Suddenly, the weight of what I was doing hit me. "What will Grace think?" I mumbled.

Blake cocked an eyebrow. "She wouldn't believe you would come home after two months in Taiwan married?"

"Blake." I gave him my best, level stare. "I grew up never doing anything my parents disapproved of."

"Well, your dad liked me. I think he'd approve of the match."

"But are my neighbors going to know you knew my dad?"

"I find it is easiest to stick as close to the truth as possible. Then you don't have to remember so many lies."

I threw up my hands. "So you know my dad from somewhere."

"Old family friends," Blake inserted. "So, we've known each other for a while but had lost contact, and we both happened to go to Taiwan at about the same time."

I studied him for a minute. "I don't know if I should be impressed or worried about being married to someone who can think of such a believable lie so easily."

"I like impressed, and I'm glad you have agreed to marry me. We could stop at a courthouse somewhere and make it official."

I glared at him.

"Sorry, bad joke."

My phone dinged. It was Luke. I hadn't texted him in a while.

Luke: Are you okay? I haven't heard from you in a while.
Me: I'm fine.

I grimaced. What would Luke think about this charade?

Me: I'm on my way home.

Luke: Let me know when you get back so I can come see you.

That could turn into an interesting conversation but wouldn't worry about it now. I bit back a smile. I'd let Blake deal with it.

"I believe that some ring-shopping is in order on the way home. None of my neighbors would believe my father would approve of someone so cheap as to not buy me a ring."

"Really? The girl who never wears any jewelry."

He had noticed that? "I need a ring to show I'm married. That is one piece of jewelry I want."

"Okay." He swung off the freeway. "Find a place."

I found a jewelry store nearby and directed Blake to it. When he grabbed my hand after opening my door, I tried to pull it back, but he held on tighter. "We're engaged or close to it. We would be holding hands."

I sighed. I didn't know about this pretend thing. Blake may have been pretending, but my body didn't know the difference. Warmth from his touch spread through my arm, and my heart skipped a couple of beats.

"Don't look so scared," Blake said.

"Stop bossing me around," I hissed, then pasted a smile on as we went into the store.

After casually admiring a few rings, I felt myself relax into the charade. Blake kept suggesting big gaudy rings I hated. I wanted simple. I pointed at a marquise-shaped diamond set in a white gold band with two smaller diamonds next to it. "That one."

I hoped it wasn't too expensive, but the rings didn't have any price tags. I shrugged. Uncle Sam was probably paying, since it was for undercover work.

"You heard the lady," Blake said to the salesman. "We want that one."

It would take a day to size it, so Blake called Agent Collins, who was staying in Salt Lake City, and asked him to pick it up.

"So, how did you propose? My neighbors will be really impressed if I tell them you just gave it to me without a word."

"What do you suggest?"

I thought of our last kiss and my cheeks warmed. That would have been a perfect setting for a proposal. Our story couldn't be something that personal if it was pretend. "Up at the Big Buddha?"

He quirked an eyebrow. "That doesn't sound very romantic."

I shrugged. I didn't want our fake engagement story to be romantic when I was angry we wouldn't have a real engagement story.

I studied him while he concentrated on the heavy traffic. He seemed different, but I couldn't place it. Less shy and more sure of himself. Had I fallen for someone who didn't even exist? The thought made my stomach drop, even though I found this Blake intriguing.

Blake noticed me staring. "What? You're not having second thoughts on the ring, are you?"

"I'm just wondering who you are."

He glanced around as if he expected to find someone else in the car. "Me?" he asked after a few seconds.

I cocked my head to the side. "Yes, you. In Taiwan, you seemed shy, even if you showed your confidence. But now..."

Blake held up a hand to cut me off. "I'm still that guy." He shrugged. "I guess I'm not shy, per se. I don't show too much of myself all at once."

"Is that why you were chosen to protect me in Taiwan? Because you're a lot like me."

He shrugged.

"So... Why you?"

"Honestly. Because of my knowledge of the country and the language, and I was close enough to your age for it to be plausible I would choose to work at the school."

"But I hadn't decided to go until three weeks before I showed up."

"Your father told us you had applied and said we needed to get you there sooner if things didn't go well in Baja. It was best an agent go work at the same school."

"Who did we replace?"

"Some teachers who got a better offer somewhere else."

Chapter 30

I was sure my heart stopped when Blake parked in front of my house. I took a deep breath, then another, but as Blake got out and retrieved a couple of suitcases, I continued to sit frozen in the car.

"Can I have the keys?" Blake asked.

I numbly handed them over.

He was at the door in a second with one hand inside his jacket, ready to pull his gun if needed. I blinked. Of course, he would want to check out the house before I went in. I continued to stare, trying with all of my might not to feel overwhelmed. It was better not to feel anything.

I jumped when Blake opened my door. "Come on. It's clear."

My body refused to move. It wasn't clear. Every emotion I had felt when my dad died was waiting for me when I stepped through the doors. I was sure of it.

Blake leaned over. "You can do it."

My breath caught, and I shook my head. I tried to not think at all, but the pain was already bubbling up. I had gone across the ocean and found a part of my independence and freedom, but I didn't want to be reminded I had no family.

Blake held out his hand. "I'll be with you." His voice was soft.

I raised my eyes to meet his. I took a deep breath and slowly put my hand in his. He helped me out of the car, wrapped his arm around my waist, and guided me to the house. A part of me wanted to fight his compassion. He had used me. But I needed some support. Blake was the only one I had right now.

My hands shook as Blake pushed the door open. The big entry was not very welcoming. It looked dark and cold.

"Come on." Blake gently propelled me forward.

I pressed against his arm around my waist. My body wanted to avoid the pain I knew lurked in these walls, but my feet moved forward. The front sitting room came into view, and Blake steered me in there.

"Sit," he said. "I'll get our stuff." He left me standing on the threshold of the room my parents only used to entertain guests. It was where I had met with Luke. It was also where my parents counseled me. It was where we sat at night, discussing our days and had family nights.

I took a few steps into the room. The family picture on the wall facing the window caught my eye. My parents smiled with their arms around each other. Their hands rested on my shoulders.

My chest crushed in on itself, and I gasped for breath. My strength left me, and I slumped to the floor. I curled up with my arms wrapped around my waist. How was I going to survive without them?

They may have not been perfect parents, but they loved me. And I loved them. I wished I had known them better, that they would have relaxed more with me, willing to hear my dreams and desires as well as holding their dreams for me. Images flashed through my mind to when I was a child. I sat next to my mom on her vanity as she got ready, begging her to put a little lipstick on me. My dad took me to art lessons because I had begged him nonstop.

My mom went with me to a nursing home to deliver the little pictures I had painted. She had talked to everyone as I shyly hid behind her back. Art was the one dream I had been brave enough to voice.

A month before my mom died, I had wanted to give my parents the best anniversary gift, to show them their investment in my art classes had been worth it. I had stood at the falls next to the temple, waiting for the sun and the colors to be perfect. I went to that spot every night for a week, taking different pictures at different times to get the perfect shot. Then I had painted that picture onto a huge canvas. I had improved a lot since then, but I was still proud of it. My mom cried when I gave it to them and said how much she loved it. She had made Dad hang it on the wall in the room where she could see it when she first woke up in the morning. Every morning for that month, she hugged me and said the picture was beautiful. I had created something that really meant something to my parents, at least to my mom. In fact, it was the first time I felt I had made a small impact in their life.

All I had were memories of them sacrificing for me.

I wanted to disappear into the floor. It was like I had lived with strangers. I had no idea what their hopes and dreams were, and they didn't really know mine.

I didn't hear Blake come back in, but I jumped when he put a hand on my arm. When I didn't move, he lay next to me and wrapped an arm around my waist, his hand resting on my arms tightly clutching my stomach. He supported his upper body with his other elbow as he watched the tears crawl down my cheeks. He didn't say anything but stroked my arm with his thumb.

I stared straight ahead, not seeing anything in the room, but his touch was reassuring and comforting.

"Do you want to lie on the couch?"

I nodded, my head rubbing against the rug on the hardwood floor. Blake helped me to the couch. He sat next to me and pulled me close.

"Do you want to talk?" he asked.

"I can't," I gasped as my body continued to shake with sobs. Blake didn't move from my side until my tears had subsided. I didn't know how long we sat there, but I watched the shadows in the room slowly shift. The tears finally dried, but I felt numb. I never wanted to feel again. I never wanted to relive this awful pain.

"I miss them so much," I managed to whisper.

"I know." His voice was gruff. I lifted my head. Even in the dim light, I could see the tears in his eyes as he met my gaze.

I searched his eyes for a moment before he pulled me closer for a hug.

"I don't like seeing you in so much pain."

An hour later, he called for delivery, and we ate in the sitting room. I almost insisted we go to the kitchen, knowing Mom would have freaked out if she knew I was eating in this room. But I knew the memories in the kitchen would be even worse.

I forced myself to give Blake a quick tour of the house and showed him the room he could stay in.

"Are you ready for bed?"

I felt like I hadn't slept for a week, but I didn't want to be alone.

"Will you stay with me until I fall asleep?"

"Of course."

Blake waited in the hall until after I changed into my pajamas, he tucked me into bed like I was a small child. I clutched his hand when I thought he was going to leave.

"I'm not going anywhere yet. I was looking for a chair."

"Just sit on my bed." I scooted from the edge to give him room.

He sat and alternated between rubbing my back and stroking my hair. I begged him to tell me about him, needing to distract myself from thinking about the fact my parents were gone.

"What do you want to know?" he asked.

"Anything."

He thought for a moment. "I grew up on a farm. I moved pipe when I was twelve and drove the tractors by the time I was fifteen. I loved to go horseback riding. I miss it." He squeezed my hand. "I'll have to take you home, and we can go for a ride."

"That could be an adventure."

"Yeah, I probably shouldn't tell you this, but I remember when I was young, maybe ten, I was riding out in the pastures. My older brother came up from behind me on a motorcycle, and the horse spooked and sidestepped. I slipped right off before I even had a chance to tighten my grip." He chuckled. "My brother had laughed and laughed, and I told him it didn't count as getting bucked off because I had landed on my feet." He leaned closer. "In my mind, real cowboys didn't get bucked off."

I smiled. "Tell me about your family."

And so he did. He talked until I finally succumbed to a blissful sleep. I was in a half-wakeful state with my eyes closed when he kissed my forehead.

"Just yell if you need me." The bed shifted as he stood. A moment later, I heard him whisper, "I love you." Or maybe I had dreamed it.

Chapter 31

When I woke up, I could hear Blake in the kitchen. I braced myself against the memories as I entered the dining room, but the memories that formed were not painful at all. The love of my parents was so strong tears sprang to my eyes. But these were happier tears than the night before. Blake must have sensed my presence and turned from the stove.

"Good morning, beautiful."

My cheeks heated, and I put my hand to my hair. I had a momentary panic as I realized I hadn't even tried to look presentable. Then I forced my hand to my side. I was pretending I was married. My husband would no doubt see me looking terrible in the morning after a hard night. My puffy eyes itched and burned. I went to the freezer, grabbed an ice pack, and held it against my face.

Blake's face creased with concern.

"Too much crying," I said to explain the ice pack.

Blake took the eggs off the stove and then stepped toward me. He held me for a long moment.

"The eggs are getting cold," I told him, confused about the surge of warmth running through my body. I appreciated his concern, but I was still smarting from his deception in Taiwan. "Where did you get them, anyway? I'm sure anything in the fridge would be bad."

"I asked for a favor, and some agents delivered some basics this morning. We'll have to go shopping today."

I let him set the table and put on breakfast while I concentrated on holding the ice pack against one eye and then the other, bringing down the swelling.

"Sorry, you are having to cook. I thought that was the wife's job."

"That's old-fashioned thinking. Husbands can cook, too, especially ones who *like* cooking."

"And you're one of those?"

He nodded.

"I guess you might be worth keeping around."

Blake grinned. "If that's what it takes, I'll cook every meal for you."

"Then what would I do?"

Blake glanced out the patio window. "It looks like we have some yard work to do."

"I hope you aren't going to make me do it myself. That might be grounds for dismissal. How about we share both jobs?" I couldn't believe I was joking and teasing with him about this very awkward situation. At least doing yardwork would give me some time to think.

"We also need to meet with your lawyer."

"Why?"

"To make sure everything with your father's company is secure."

"I did that before I left, but he will definitely want to meet you. I'll call him."

Blake's eyebrows shot up. "He works on Saturday?"

I shook my head and retrieved my phone as he washed the dishes.

I ignored Blake's questioning gaze as I dialed Luke's number.

"Alia?" Luke's voice was full of concern, and I almost started crying again.

"Hey, Luke." I hid a smile as Blake's mouth dropped open. I guessed Luke being like an uncle was not on my profile. "I made it home from Taiwan."

"And you're okay?" he asked.

"Well, I'm still alive. A lot happened my last day there." I didn't know why I was so self-conscious with Blake listening in.

"And?"

What should I say? Blake said we both needed to meet with him, but would he meet with Blake? "Umm, well, I got married and thought we should probably all meet together."

"You what?" Luke's voice was low. But before I could think of a response, he went on. "I'll be there at one."

"It can wait until Monday."

"No, it can't." He hung up.

I shrugged at Blake. "Good luck."

My smile broadened at Blake's baffled look. Luke would put him in his place, and I found satisfaction in the thought. Some payback for his deceit.

After breakfast, I went out to clean the dead foliage out of flower beds so the new flowers could grow in. Blake started cleaning the leaves out of the rain gutters.

"I thought I saw you come home."

I jumped, landing on my bum. I looked up into the bright old eyes of my neighbor. Grace's wrinkled face shone with pleasure. Her brown eyes glinted with a hint of mischievousness.

I remembered her getting hit in the head.

"I heard some guy trying to get into my house knocked you out. Are you okay?"

"It takes a lot more than a bump on the head to take out this old biddy."

I chuckled.

"Sorry, I didn't get your flowerbeds cleaned out. It's good to see you." Her eagerness to change the subject suggested she was pretending to be braver than she felt. She glanced around. "I noticed you have a man with you." Her eyebrows raised in question.

"I got married." I searched the backyard for him, but Blake was still in the front.

She looked pointedly at my left hand.

"I didn't want to wear my ring while doing yard work," I lied. I couldn't tell her an FBI agent would deliver it later.

She strode through the gate that separated our backyards before I could get to my feet.

"You eloped while you were in Taiwan?"

"Well, technically, we got married when we got back to the States."

I wished Blake would have a reason to come to the backyard soon. He needed to be here to answer these questions. We had to keep our story straight.

"You didn't think I would want to come to your wedding? You're like a grandchild to me."

I could see the doubt in her eyes. Blake rounded the corner of the house, and I waved at him. "You need to meet him."

"Darn right, I do," she muttered under her breath.

I stifled a laugh. I felt bad that she thought I got married without inviting her, but her grumpy attitude was comical.

Blake made his way over.

Grace nudged me. "Well, I gotta say you have good taste. He's good-looking. He's a hard worker as well."

Blake put his arm around me. "Is this the neighbor you told me about?"

Grace beamed. I had to give it to Blake. He knew how to turn an awkward situation around.

Grace extended her hand. "Grace Little, but call me Grace. No Ms. Little or Sister Little for me." She released Blake's hand and gestured to herself. "I mean, who wants to be told they are little when they are as tall as I am?"

Blake and I laughed. Grace was almost six feet.

"Alia was just telling me you guys eloped when you got back to the States."

I breathed a sigh of relief, grateful I didn't have to communicate that tidbit of information before he said something contrary.

"We did. I'm sorry we didn't tell anyone. We'll have a ceremony later for friends."

"What was the hurry?" She glanced from my face down to my midsection, and then her steely eyes met Blake's.

My stomach lurched. I had agreed to pretend to be married because I didn't believe Grace would believe I would sleep with a man I wasn't married to. Would everyone think I got married in a rush because I was pregnant?

Blake put a hand on Grace's shoulder. "You don't need to worry about anything. I couldn't part from her. I fell in love with her in Taiwan but didn't want to go back to Texas where I was working without her. So, we decided to get married."

"Why not just quit and get your own place here and give yourself some time?"

I stepped forward. "When you know something is right, there's no use waiting."

"I see." Grace glared at Blake before smiling at me. "Church starts at 10:30. I would love if you sat next to me. Your family always did. I've been feeling a bit lonely since…" She cleared her throat. "Anyway. I'll see you Sunday?"

"We'll sit by you, Grace." I forced the words past the lump in my throat. I didn't want to go to church with a new husband to introduce, but I couldn't let down Grace. "Thanks for caring for the house while I was gone."

"Oh, I loved it. I felt like a real spy, keeping watch out my bedroom window or from my back patio. I don't think the people trying to clean the windows even knew I was there." She leaned closer. "I think the FBI should hire me. No one would suspect this old biddy."

Blake coughed, though it sounded like he was covering up a laugh.

"Anyway… I really appreciated knowing someone was watching out for my parents' home." Tears spilled over. Blake tightened his hold on me.

Grace hugged both Blake and me, since Blake was already holding me. "Oh honey, your mom was my best friend—more like a daughter I never had. She made me promise to look after you and give you some matronly influence. I could never let anything happen to your home while you were gone."

"You have been more like a grandmother to me."

Blake's phone rang, and he excused himself.

I gave Grace a final hug, and she pointed at Blake. "I'll be watching him."

Chapter 32

Agent Collins was in the house when I went inside. Blake held up my ring and grinned.

"Special delivery," Agent Collins said.

Blake handed me the ring, and I slid it on. It fit perfectly.

"You better think of a good story of how you proposed," I said bitterly. My anger toward Blake was diminishing, but it was still there. Grace's obvious thought I might be pregnant also hurt. "The neighbors might want to hear about it if they don't assume I'm pregnant first."

I fled to my room. I had to get a hold of my emotions before Luke came.

Blake knocked on my door and opened it a crack. "Can I come in?"

I didn't say anything, so Blake must have taken it as permission. He sat on the edge of the bed and rubbed my back.

"I'm sorry, Alia. I really am."

I glanced at the clock, not wanting to talk about it. "Luke will be here in an hour. We better eat some lunch."

Blake sighed and stood, then waited for me to sit up and held out his hand to help me. I took his hand, but he held tight when I attempted to pull away.

"Alia. I'm really sorry. Maybe everyone won't assume you're pregnant."

I nodded because I didn't know what else to say. He was right. I didn't know everyone would make that assumption. If everyone believed the story about us being family friends, then it would make sense, but we had missed saying that to Grace. I determined to make sure I included that tidbit if asked.

Luke Douglas rang the doorbell a few minutes before one o'clock.

Blake beat me to the door and then immediately offered his hand. "Hello, sir. I'm Blake Hansen, Alia's husband."

Luke took Blake's hand and held on a moment longer than necessary, his lips in a grim line. "Luke Douglas. I'm like a second father to Alia, as well her lawyer."

Understanding dawned in Blake's features.

"I'd like to talk to Alia privately." Luke's tone was firm. He hardly even tried to keep a professional attitude.

"I'll wait on the back porch," Blake said. "Just let me know when you are ready." Blake left, and Luke followed him. I followed along, worried Luke would do something crazy, but he just locked the door behind Blake. Blake didn't even react to the sound of the lock sliding into place, and I had to admit he was a good actor.

Luke took my arm and led me to the sitting room.

"You're married?" Luke asked as soon as we sat.

I nodded, afraid if I spoke, he would see right through the lie.

Luke studied me for several minutes before breaking the silence. "I find it hard to believe you would get married without telling anyone about it."

I wished Blake was here. I couldn't lie to Luke, but I didn't want to blow Blake's cover.

He studied me for a long time. Finally, he took a deep breath and leaned forward, resting his elbows on his knees.

"You remember I told you about Frank Barlow?"

"Yes." I couldn't tell him I had had plenty of conversations with the FBI.

"I told you your father was doing contracted work for CORE-TECH with their financing to dig oil off the coast of the Baja. I found documents in your father's computers. He had in a letter that he wanted me to check them if something happened to him. Your father figured out it was a cover to explain large amounts of money transferring from the account. He went to the FBI and told them his suspicions and insisted he would help them uncover information. A couple of weeks before your father's death, your father found information the

FBI needed. He knew it would be dangerous. As a precaution, before he left, he met with me to get everything in order."

I nodded, remembering too late Luke wouldn't know I knew all this. But I had told Luke the FBI was in Taiwan with me. At my lack of reaction, Luke raised his eyebrows.

"Alia. I found some information in your father's notes on his computer. I fear I found why Frank had him killed. Do you want me to bring in Blake? I assume he'll want to hear this."

He had already figured out the charade. It didn't surprise me. Luke seemed to read any situation in less than a minute and figure out the truth. Without waiting for an answer, Luke got up and left me alone.

I heard him open the back door and tell Blake to come in.

Luke offered his hand to Blake when they got back into the room. "FBI?"

Blake shot a look at me as he shook Luke's hand.

"She didn't say anything. I figured it out. She told me FBI were watching her in Taiwan."

Blake sat stiffly next to me.

"If you are here, I'm guessing you aren't really married, but you're protecting her."

"Yes, sir. So far, my superiors haven't been able to find Frank Barlow. He keeps sending others to do his dirty work. With the attacks on Alia, the FBI thought it imperative I come with her."

Worry creased Luke's forehead. I had told him about the attacks, but I guessed hearing it from Blake made it more real. "I was telling Alia I found more information you might want to know, though you might already know it."

Luke returned his gaze to me. "Your father found out that Frank was smuggling jewels. I'm assuming since his company is based in the United States, even though they sometimes do 'work' outside the United States, their home base near their Baja drilling is southern California." He glanced at Blake, who nodded. Even I knew about the embezzling. I decided not to tell Luke that.

"Your father sent the final evidence to a separate secure email the day before he died."

Blake's back straightened.

Luke glanced at Blake. "Do you have a laptop?"

"Yes." Blake retrieved his laptop and after accessing the email, Blake typed something on the computer, then shut it. Then he tapped something on his phone. I figured he forwarded the email to someone and had let them know.

"My main priority is keeping Alia safe." Blake lifted his phone to his ear and after a moment said. "Come to the house."

After he hung up, he turned to us. "Frank probably caught wind he had sent the information, and that is why he had Alia's father killed."

My hand tightened its grip on Blake's and only then did I realize I was holding it. Someone knocked on the door, and Blake let in Agent Collins.

Blake took up the story once Agent Collins was settled. "So after that threat was taken care of, he went after your father's money, probably to convince people your father was in financial trouble and thus lied in the email he sent. Which is why he sent someone to Taiwan." Blake turned to me.

"Because we moved the money," I added. "Would my life even be in danger if I had left the money alone?"

"Maybe," Blake admitted. "But then Frank would have disappeared, and it would be harder to find him."

"As much as I hate the idea, Alia…" Luke's eyes were soft and compassionate. "You are doing a great service helping the FBI catch this guy. This guy is willing to kill to get what he wants. But since your father made sure Frank wouldn't be able to access the money that really belongs to you and the funds that really belong to his company, Frank is probably furious." Luke touched my knee. "I'm worried about you."

I gave him a small smile. "I'll be fine. Blake's here to protect me."

Luke continued to study me. I could see the worry, and I forced myself not to show how scared I was.

I turned to Blake. "They haven't found anything on Frank Barlow?"

"No."

I stood. "Thank you for everything, Luke. I'll let you know if I need anything else."

Luke gave me a tight hug. He shook Blake's hand and held onto it until Blake met his hard stare.

"I better not hear of you doing anything out of line while you are pretending to be her husband. Her father was like a brother to me, so I feel responsible for her."

Blake smiled easily. "You don't have to worry about anything. I'll take care of her."

Luke left and Blake led Agent Collins to the front door. I heard them conversing in low voices but couldn't make out their words.

I stood with my arms folded when Blake came back into the room. Now that it was getting too hot to work in the yard, I didn't know what to do. I felt awkward with Blake in my house.

Blake stood in front of me. He reached out to me, but then stopped himself and stuffed his hands in his pockets. "Ali. I don't blame you for not trusting me."

"Tell me what happened." I paused. When Blake looked confused, I clarified. "In Baja. You said on the plane you would tell me later."

"From what we can determine, Frank went with your father on a yacht, probably saying that it was a way to 'wine and dine' him. By the time the FBI figured out where they were, it was too late."

I nodded once, my throat burning.

"So Frank killed him?"

"There were several other people on board, so no, we don't know that for sure."

"How much do you know about me?" I asked, wanting to know how much he was pretending and how much info he spouted was memorized from some kind of profile.

"A lot," Blake said. "But I didn't know what a caring person you are until I met you. While in Taiwan, I learned how kind and thoughtful you are. You gave your love to your students freely. You are one of the strongest people I know. After all you went through in Taiwan, you are still sticking it out." He paused and stepped closer. "I know you felt something for me, and I'm hoping you can feel that way again." He paused and lowered his voice. "Did that answer your question?"

I swallowed twice before I found my voice. "Yeah."

I clutched Blake's hand as we entered church the next day. I wasn't sure why I was depending on him for support, since he was the reason this was going to be so uncomfortable. We sat next to Grace. With every person I introduced Blake to, I tried to say we were old family friends, and to my surprise, they didn't act as if me getting married was strange at all. They welcomed Blake warmly and said they were so glad I had made it home safely.

The bishop requested to meet with us, so we agreed.

"Bishop Clayton," the bishop said, extending his hand to Blake before shaking my hand.

I sat awkwardly. I wondered if I would be forced to lie to the bishop. I hoped Blake would answer the hard questions.

Bishop Clayton studied Blake for a long time. "You know you can trust me to keep anything said here confidential. Who are you?"

Blake sighed. "I'm an FBI agent. Alia's life is in danger. She was almost kidnapped several times in Taiwan. I came with her to protect her. But I do love her and would love to really marry her."

I glanced at Blake. He studied me intently, and I saw he meant what he said. He hadn't lied to the bishop. My chest tightened. I wanted to believe him, but the hurt was still there, somewhere deep inside.

"Alia?" Bishop Clayton's words broke through my thoughts. "Would you like a blessing?"

Relief spread through my body. I hadn't even thought of that. "Please."

After the blessing, peace infused my body. Something the bishop said rolled around in my mind on the way home. He had said to trust Heavenly Father, but he also blessed I would be able to trust Blake. I knew there was no way the bishop would have known I didn't trust him.

Once we parked, Blake walked around the car as I stood there, fighting the swirl of emotions. Trust him? Could I? I trusted him to protect me, but that was different than trusting my heart with him again.

"Let's go for a walk," Blake suggested.

I took his offered hand. "Can we change first?"

Blake grinned. "I think I would prefer that."

After we changed, Blake offered me his arm and locked the door. My hand rested comfortably on his arm. As we walked along the road in silence, my confusion worsened. I didn't want to trust him with my heart. At least not yet. I concentrated on the open space around where I lived. My parents' house was far enough from the city that there were not a lot of houses near us.

"Blake? How can I?"

"How can you what?"

"Trust you."

"I know I hurt you. It breaks my heart to see you hurting. But I meant everything I said. I do love you."

I rubbed at my face. "I guess this is what happens when you've never had a boyfriend before." How could I know his love was real?

Blake lifted his eyebrows. "I'm the first?"

"That wasn't on my profile." I couldn't help smiling.

Blake shook his head.

"Are you my boyfriend?" I asked.

"No, I'm your husband." He took my hand from his arm and held it in his. "But I like to think you were my girlfriend before we left Taiwan."

We would have been boyfriend and girlfriend still if Blake hadn't broken my trust. His actions spoke of his feelings for me, but I couldn't get myself to trust those feelings. I couldn't open myself to the inevitable heartache after the FBI caught Frank and Blake left for his next assignment.

We walked along in silence for a while longer. Blake seemed content to leave me to my thoughts. He gripped my hand as though he was afraid to let me go. He glanced at me several times but never spoke.

The familiar flame of attraction shot through my body at his touch and attention. I tried to squelch it, but Blake was hard to resist. Despite wanting him to go far away after they caught Frank, I found myself secretly wishing we were really married. But I wanted Blake to earn my affection... at least a little.

We got back to the house, and Blake locked the door behind us as we entered the foyer. He led me into the sitting room and gently pulled me next to him. He wrapped his arms around me and held me. His hands rubbed up and down my arms slowly, sending shivers of pleasure running through my limbs. The constant touch soothed me, and I relaxed. Slowly my eyes closed, and I let myself enjoy the moment with no thoughts of the future.

Chapter 33

I was getting chased again, but this time I couldn't see my attacker. The buildings around me were unfamiliar. I staggered through dark streets, my heart racing, certain the person after me would suddenly appear. I turned a corner, and a man stood at the end of the dead-end street. It was Frank Barlow. He took a step toward me. I stumbled backward, but another pair of arms grabbed me from behind.

I gasped as I sat upright in bed. Forcing the images out of my mind, I took deep breaths. I was safe. Blake was here. There was no immediate threat.

It was five in the morning, but there was no way I was going back to sleep now.

I grabbed my sketch pad I had taken to Taiwan and crept up the stairs to a room I had not been in since my parents died. I slowly twisted the doorknob and cringed at the screech the door made as I swung it open. Several times I would try to escape here to paint through my grief at my mother's death, but that squeaky door would always lead my father to me. Then I would feel the need to pretend I wasn't hurting just like he was.

There, as I had left it, was my art studio. Easels were set up with canvases on them, waiting for me to create beautiful scenes on them. One half-finished painting caught my eye. It was the one I had been working on when I found out my father had died. Trying for a sort of impressionistic painting, I had used the dots to create my mom's favorite flowers in such a way that my mom's face appeared in the center without her actually being there. An invisible pull to finish the painting overwhelmed me.

I took a deep breath, inhaling the scent of paints and charcoal. My fingertips barely grazed the surface of the easels as I touched them, afraid to disturb the serenity I felt there.

I fingered the oil paints, charcoal pencils, and paint brushes, suddenly itching to work on a project. I had planned to paint a picture from my sketch pad, but I glanced again at the painting sitting undisturbed on the easel. I needed to finish it, for me. It differed from my other oil paintings I had done, and I was challenged by it.

I opened the window to let in some air and sat down.

I mixed a few paints and got started, painting dots of color, enriching the picture, and adding depth to it. The shade of the colors shifted with the rising sun, but I barely noticed the passage of time.

"Ali?"

I jumped at the panic in Blake's voice.

"Up here," I called back, not even turning around. I didn't want to stop.

"That's looking great, Alia." Blake's voice came from the open door.

"Thanks." I didn't even turn to look at him as I concentrated on the last few dots on one of the irises I was working on. The peach of the flower gave the illusion of the flesh of my mother's face.

"When did you come up here?"

"About five. I had a bad dream and couldn't go back to sleep."

"I thought you were sleeping in until I noticed your door was open, and I didn't see you in there."

"I'm sorry I caused you concern."

"It's okay. I'm just glad you weren't kidnapped right from under my nose." He rested his hands on the back of my chair.

"It's a beautiful picture." He gestured to the sketch pad I had brought up with me. "May I?"

"Go ahead."

He opened to the picture I had sketched from Cijin Island. I had added Blake to the picture after my first night home, when Blake had been so attentive. In the sketch, Blake sat beside me, his arm around me.

"This was the moment I thought I might be in trouble," he said.

"What do you mean?" I stretched my back and started cleaning my brushes.

"I knew I felt more than was professional." He paused, making me look at him. "It was the moment I realized I loved you."

My eyes widened. "You had only known me a month." I stood to put the brushes away.

"I know," he whispered.

His voice was full of passion. I turned to find his face inches from mine. The static between us was palpable. I breathed him in, and he seemed to do the same. My body moved closer, and I rested my hand on his chest, unable to resist touching him, reassuring myself this tension was real.

His heart thumped under my palm. He was feeling it, too. I focused my gaze on his chest for a moment before raising my gaze. His blue eyes were dark, studying me with an intensity that made me catch my breath.

He glanced at my lips. I wanted him to kiss me but knew he wouldn't push, especially since I insisted I couldn't trust him, but something about this felt right. I lifted my chin slightly, letting him know I wanted him to kiss me. I wrapped my arms around his neck. My lips were inches from his.

"Alia," he murmured before lightly touching his lips to mine. I could tell he was trying to resist, which made me want him more. I caressed my lips against his, barely letting my lips touch his, yet wanting to feel the tantalizing softness of him.

He wrapped his arms around my waist, pulled my body against his, and his lips grew hungry on mine. Warmth flowed through my veins. I wanted to stay like this, to forget that someone might want to kill me and to forget that I was only pretending Blake was my husband.

I pulled back breathless, needing to clear my mind.

"Ali." Blake's voice was thick with emotion. "Please tell me this means you'll give me a chance."

"After this mess with Frank is over... I'll try."

"Ali, I love you." He grabbed my left hand where my ring should be, but I hadn't put it on before I came to paint. "I want to put a ring on this finger for real and get to be with you forever."

To my embarrassment, tears leaked out of my eyes. He said he loved me, and after that kiss, I believed him, but I held back. The pain of his deceit in Taiwan still demanded attention. But I knew I was holding onto a grudge, and lying about my feelings for him wouldn't heal that pain.

"When we put this mess with Frank behind us, I'll be able to think about the future." I put my hand on his cheek, wanting to protect my heart. How would I know for sure? The prospect was terrifying, yet electrifying all at once.

It had been three weeks since we returned home, and we hadn't heard anything about Frank or seen anybody lurking about the house. I was sure they had given up, but Blake still insisted we go everywhere together. I enjoyed associating with others at church, but other than that, we only went out to the grocery store. The rest of the time, we were at home. I could tell Blake was nervous about going places. I assumed it was because it was harder to protect me in crowds.

Over the last week, however, the walls had closed in on me, and I felt a tremendous urge to visit my parents. I needed their counsel. And even if they couldn't answer, I could voice my concerns aloud. The problem was, it was about my feelings for Blake, and I didn't want him to overhear. It was Thursday. People would be at work if I went in the middle of the day. It wouldn't be crowded and Agent Collins could follow behind.

I found Blake working on his computer in the kitchen.

"Blake?" I fiddled with my hands. "I want to go visit my parents."

Blake nodded. "I can go right now if you want."

"Well, the thing is. I..." I paused. "Please don't take this the wrong way, but I need to talk to them alone... about you."

Blake's eyebrows rose. "Alia. It isn't safe yet."

"I know. Agent Collins can follow me."

Blake sighed. "You're right. Maybe this will help us know if he is still watching. I'll call Agent Collins."

"Thank you, Blake." I kissed him lightly on the cheek.

"Promise me you'll be careful."

"I promise."

He brushed his finger across my cheek, moving a stray hair. "I hope talking to them about me helps."

I turned to get the keys to my mom's car so Blake wouldn't see the heat rising to my cheeks.

Taking the long way to the cemetery gave me time to figure out what I wanted to say.

I parked and wandered over to my parents' grave. I kneeled in front of the headstone, expecting the grief to overwhelm me, but instead, a calm came over me.

"I know you always wanted me to project the perfect image, and that you loved me, but I realize now I was suffocating, unable to really be me. I love you and miss you, but I hope you will be happy for me as I move forward with my life." I paused, fingering the letters engraved on the stone.

"Mom? I think I'm in love, but I'm so scared to open my heart to him. I feel so betrayed. I know you would try to help me see my problem logically, but you can't solve problems of the heart with logic." Warmth enveloped me. I pretended it was my mom. It was the answer I was looking for.

I left the cemetery and drove down roads at random. Should I tell Blake I loved him now or wait? If I waited, would Blake give up on me? I pulled into the dunes near Sandy Downs. It was a place I went to when I was younger and needed some space from home to think.

I carried my sandals as I hiked up the first dune. Agent Collins pulled in next to my car. I stood at the top and stared out at the many houses being built. My eyes wandered to the hills in the distance, wanting to find something that would help me clear the thoughts running through my mind. I knew what I needed and even wanted to do, but fear still held me in place. The fear didn't make sense. I knew how Blake felt. I would have to act on what I knew in my heart was right, despite the fear.

He was a good man, and I believed he really loved me, despite and even because of what had happened in Taiwan.

My eyes burned and begged the tears to come, so I could feel some relief from the emotional turmoil running through me. I took a few steps down the other side of the dune, knowing I was stalling. I breathed deeply. I would walk down this dune, drive home, and tell Blake how I felt.

Tires squealed. I ran the few feet back to the top of the dune to see Agent Collins' car send gravel flying as he drove away. Another car was ahead of him. Was that Frank?

I hunkered down on top of the dune. Should I run to my car or stay put?

Another car pulled next to my car. Frank Barlow got out of the car.

Frank Barlow? But if he was here, then who was Agent Collins chasing? A blond guy climbed out the passenger door, and I gasped. How did Bridger get here? I studied the blond, my breathing raspy. It couldn't be, but a wind whipped up and blew sand into my eyes, making it hard to see. They talked for a minute, Frank gesturing wildly with his arms. They turned and seemed to look straight at me. Adrenaline shot through me. They'd recognize me easily. I sprinted down the dune and up the next one, desperate to put some distance between me and the men. I slid over the dune and held my breath, waiting for the sound of their vehicle driving away. An ominous silence weighed on me.

I grappled for my cell phone. I breathed a sigh of relief; that it was still in my pocket.

"Blake," I whispered, tears coursing down my cheeks. "Agent Collins drove off chasing a car, but now Bridger's here and Frank…"

"I'm already on my way. Daniel called," Blake interrupted.

It took me a second to remember that Daniel was Agent Collins. "Who is Agent Collins chasing?"

"He said it was Frank."

Rough hands grabbed my arm, and I screamed.

Chapter 34

I threw a handful of sand behind me, hoping to hit my attacker. The guy swore and released me. I clutched onto my phone like a lifeline and sprinted down the hill. The guy at the top of the dune rubbed furiously at his eyes. It wasn't Bridger. But the resemblance made it clear he was a relative.

I ran away, keeping my eyes on the Bridger look-alike. Then I ran into something solid, and arms gripped me like a vice. It was Frank. "Alia. If you just come with me, I won't hurt you. You can give me what I want, and I'll let you go."

"You're not getting anything from me," I spat. I kicked as I struggled to free myself from his hold.

He dragged me around the dune.

I screamed and kicked, my elbows pinned next to my body. Frank was a lot stronger than I expected the older man to be.

"Tell me how to get the money."

"You'll kill me, anyway. You killed my father."

"Not until I get what I want." He tightened his grip when I slipped out of his hands.

New hope reared inside of me. I kicked at his legs and my foot connected with his knee. He cried out and dropped me.

I was on my feet in an instant and ran toward the end of the dune. Scanning the area for the Bridger look-alike, I spotted him on top of the dune as he pulled out a gun.

I dove behind the shallow end of the next mountain of sand. A shot rang out and sand three feet to my left kicked up. I scrambled around the dune, desperate to keep the mountain of sand between us.

"Don't kill her. She's our key," Frank yelled.

I sprinted toward the next mountain, knowing I would soon reach the brush area that separated the dunes from the racing track.

"Alia. Stop. Or I'll shoot." The Bridger look-alike was right behind me.

I froze.

He strode toward me, and I frantically tried to think of something. The guy aimed his gun at me. I would have to wait for another opportunity. If I fought back now, the guy would surely shoot me. Frank had said not to kill me, but that didn't mean this guy wouldn't shoot. The guy's eyes were bloodshot, and sand stuck to his face.

He grabbed my arm and shoved the gun into my side, making me gasp.

This was it. I was going to die. I had no doubt Blake would make sure they didn't get the money, that they paid for their crimes, but I was going to die before I had a chance to tell Blake I loved him.

"You'll pay for that little trick." He brought the gun up and hit me in the side of the head. Lights exploded in my vision, and I slumped before I regained my balance, shaking my head and fighting to stay conscious. He pushed me forward.

"I won't give you what you want." My words surprised even me. I didn't want to die, but something inside of me snapped. They would kill me after they got access to the money, anyway. I would not give this guy or Frank Barlow anything. And I wasn't going anywhere with him, either.

I let every muscle in my body go limp, imitating dead weight. The guy pitched sideways and lost his footing in the shifting sand. I kicked the gun. It flew out of his hand and landed a few yards away. I leaped for the gun, but his rough hand caught my wrist and dragged me down. He lunged forward, tackling me. He grabbed the gun and pushed my chest into the sand, pulling my hair to lift my head and pressing the gun into my back.

"Try that again and I don't care what my uncle says, you're dead."

My body trembled as tears continued to flow. I couldn't fight anymore. He hoisted me up and, keeping a firm grip around my middle, pushed me forward to walk the best we could around the dune.

"Let her go!"

The guy whirled around, holding me in front of him. He pressed the gun to my head.

Agent Collins lay on the top of a dune, his gun out.

"Help!" I shrieked.

The guy holding me swung the gun in Agent Collins' direction and shot. Agent Collins ducked at the same time something hit the guy hard from behind. We both lurched forward, and he landed on me, knocking the wind out of me. I pushed to get away from him, but his grip tightened and he pressed my face into the sand.

He suddenly let go and rolled. I twisted my head and scrambled backward. Blake was on top of the guy, wrestling to get control. A few punches landed, then Blake managed to turn him over, twist his arm behind his back, and press him into the sand. Agent Collins ran up and cuffed the guy.

I panted and spit sand. Where was Frank? I scanned the area.

"Did you see Frank?" I asked.

Blake stood. "Where was he?"

I pointed to where I had last seen him. "On the other side of that dune."

Blake cast a worried glance at me, then sprinted around the dune. He came back a moment later. "I don't see him. We've got to get you out of here."

Blake strode over to me and helped me up.

The tears started to flow as Blake took my hand and spoke. "How close is backup?"

I had assumed he had been talking to Agent Collins, but they were both silent for a moment, apparently listening to a reply I couldn't hear. The only sound I heard was the guy, cuffed and cursing into the dirt.

"Come on, Alia. We need to get you out of here. Frank wouldn't have gone far." Blake tugged me forward, and I fell into step, jogging next to him. Now I was grateful for the exercise I had done in Taiwan. My lungs burned with the effort. He scanned the area, and then met my eyes. Frank's car was gone. Agent Collins was behind us pushing the blond guy ahead of him.

"Daniel. Let's get that guy in your car. You can take him in, and I'll take Alia home."

The attacker kicked and fought against Agent Collins' hold. Blake let go of me and grabbed the guy by his other arm. Agent Collins held one arm and Blake held another as they dragged him to Agent Collins' car. I followed close behind, casting furtive glances around the area. I had no doubt Blake was right. Frank was not far away.

Blake helped Agent Collins put the blond guy in the car, then Agent Collins drove away. I stepped toward my car when movement at the top of the nearest dune caught my eye.

"Blake!" I cried as another man ducked behind the far side of the dune.

Blake took position behind my mom's car. "Get in my car, Alia."

My hands shook as I wrenched the door open, and then slammed it shut. Blake crept around the car, keeping his gun aimed at the spot we had seen the man on the dunes.

"We'll come back later for your car." Blake put the car in reverse and stomped on the gas, yanking the steering wheel to drive away from the dunes.

I wasn't worried about my mom's car so much as I was about the presence of yet another person. Blake said something about the guy hiding in the dunes, but said we were safely away.

A few seconds, later Blake cursed softly, glancing in the rearview mirror. I spun to see what he was watching. "Don't turn around." He turned the car sharply, causing me to lean over the center console as I groped for something to steady myself. "Get down!" He yelled right before the rear window exploded.

Sharp pain lanced through my shoulder and arm. My heart stopped. I had been shot. Trying to ignore the pain, I folded myself in half to make myself disappear.

I hardly registered Blake's voice until he said my name.

"Ali, where are we?"

I raised my head long enough to get my bearings and screamed as a car almost careened into us when Blake barreled through a stop sign.

"Where, Ali?" he shouted over the sound of screeching tires and revving engines.

"49th South. East of Sand Creek Golf Course," I shouted.

Blake repeated our position. How long would it take before help arrived?

I silently pled with my Heavenly Father to let us live through this. *Please don't let anything happen to Blake or me.* I prayed. *I can't lose him now.*

Stinging pain shot through my shoulder and left arm. Drops slid down my side. I kept myself folded in half and didn't dare inspect anything.

Blake cranked the steering wheel, and my body rammed into the door. Horns blared. Blake determinedly kept his attention on the rearview mirror. Gunshots reverberated again. The mirror next to Blake's window exploded, and I screamed.

"The FBI is closing in on them, Ali," Blake said in a deceptively calm voice. His eyes met mine, fear flashing through them.

We were nearing the foothills when I heard more shots, and two cars drove past us. A loud pop snapped outside the windows, followed by a crunching sound. I jumped and spun around, sending blinding, sharp pain through my arm. The car behind us flipped once before landing upright again.

Cars surrounded the wreckage. Blake slowed and pulled over. "Are you okay?"

I stared at him, my vision tunneling. My whole body shook, and my breaths came in raspy gasps. Wet rivulets ran down my arm. Blackness was closing in.

Blake reached over and undid my seatbelt. He sprinted around to open my door.

His eyes swept over my body until his gaze landed on my arm. "You were shot." Blake helped me sit, kneeled next to me, and called for an ambulance, holding me tightly. I leaned into Blake, and the tears started anew.

"Shhh. You're safe now."

I craned my neck to look at the wrecked car, but a red stain smeared on Blake's shirt caught my attention. I stared at it in confusion.

Blake picked me up. "Come on. We gotta get you to the hospital. You're going into shock."

I clutched his shirt with my good arm. "You'll stay with me, right?" He had remained with me in the hospital in Taiwan; I needed him again.

"I will never leave you, Ali." He kissed my forehead and helped me stand.

I refused to let go of his hand. Blake climbed into the ambulance before the blackness afforded a blessed relief from the pain and the trauma of the day.

Chapter 35

When I woke up, my entire body felt stiff. I was in a boring hospital room with my left arm bandaged. Pain shot through my arm when I moved to sit up. I inhaled sharply, then groaned as I relaxed against the pillows.

"Ali?"

I smiled at the sound of Blake's voice and spotted him sitting in a chair next to the window. "You're still here."

"I told you I wouldn't leave you." He pulled the chair close to the bed and grasped my good hand.

I focused on his face, tears clouding my vision. The memories of the dunes rushed back to me. I could have died. "Is it over?"

Blake swept my hair out of my face. "We got Frank. It's all over."

"I love you," I whispered.

His eyes widened. "Really?" He cocked his head to the side, studying me. "You're not just saying that because I managed not to kill you in a car chase?"

I chuckled. "I've loved you for a while. I didn't want to admit it, especially after I felt so betrayed. I'm sorry… about everything."

"I'm sorry I couldn't tell you who I was sooner. I'm just glad you're okay."

I winced as more pain tore through my arm.

Blake pushed the nurse button.

"Was I really shot?"

"The bullet went through, but you lost quite a bit of blood."

"How long was I out?"

"Overnight."

I groaned and leaned my head against the pillow.

"You'll be getting out of here today," he reassured me.

"I'm going to hold you to that," I teased.

He leaned over and kissed me. "Good."

After they released me, and on our way home, Blake filled me in on what happened to Frank.

"Frank is in the ICU. We're not sure he will live, but we're hoping he will admit to something. Turns out the brother who worked for your dad is his twin. That was who Agent Collins went chasing after before I told him Frank was really at the dunes. We arrested the brother, and Riley Sanders—the guy you thought was Bridger—is in custody. He says he'll testify against his uncle for a lighter sentence, but we'll see what happens."

"Is he Anthony's brother?" I asked.

"No, Riley is the twin's son. Anthony's mom was a sister to Frank. Apparently, she didn't have any idea what her brother was up to."

Blake helped me out of the car when we got home. My mother's car sat in the driveway.

Blake answered my question before I could ask it. "I had Agent Collins get your mom's car."

Grace hurried over from her front yard.

"What happened?" she demanded.

"It's a long story," Blake said as he opened the front door. "Where do you want to go, Ali?"

"The couch is fine for now."

"Ali, huh?" Grace cocked an eyebrow at me. "Seems to me the only person your mom allowed to call you that was your dad."

I smiled, but a sharp, familiar pain stabbed my chest. I missed my mom more now than when she first died and Dad insisted we needed to move on. I knew now he was running from his own grief. He had poured himself into his work and even helped the FBI uncover a jewel embezzling operation. For the first time since his death, I understood why my father had done what he did. He wanted to do what little he could to make the world better. He wanted to forget that the love of his life was gone. I leaned on the couch as all the hurt and anger I had been feeling toward my dad in the years since my mother's death melted away, and tears flowed down my cheeks.

"Are you hurting?" Blake asked.

I opened my eyes and shook my head slightly. "I'm good."

It wasn't until after Grace had cooked us dinner that Blake was able to convince her she had done enough and could go home.

"What's wrong?" Blake sat next to me, taking my hand in his.

"Nothing's wrong."

"Then why were you crying earlier if you weren't hurting?"

"I just realized my father had been running away from his own grief and that was why he had acted as he did sometimes. He was protecting me from a real threat toward the end. He gave his life doing his part to make this world a better place."

"You're a lot like him that way."

"What?" I asked.

"I saw you with those kids, and I see your bravery and resilience every day."

My cheeks warmed, and I ducked my head, unable to meet his eyes. I didn't feel very resilient. I remember being scared just as much, if not more than I remembered being brave.

Blake rested his fingers under my chin and lifted my face. "Ali, getting to know you has been the best thing that has ever happened to me." Blake's smile grew bigger, and he chuckled. "I remember when you drew a stick figure of me. I couldn't resist falling for you after that."

I groaned. "That was my first day there."

Blake pulled me close. He studied me for a moment before he spoke.

"Did you mean what you said in the hospital?"

"That I love you?" I nodded. "I did mean it. I've been trying to deny it, but it's true."

Blake kneeled next to the couch and held my ring up for me to see. I hadn't even noticed it was gone. He must have taken it off at the hospital for safekeeping. "So, will you marry me? This time you can have an actual wedding."

Something between a sob and a laugh escaped my lips. "Yes."

He slid the ring on my finger and gently pulled me into his arms and held me. I leaned my head on his shoulder and breathed slowly, aware that sobbing for joy would only cause my injury to hurt.

He kissed my hair, then moved his lips slowly down my jawline until his lips found mine. I clutched his shirt with my good hand, holding him close. I pressed into him, deepening the kiss, letting him know he was all I ever wanted. His hands found my waist; the tension in them told me he wanted to pull me to him but was holding back, aware of my bruised body. I released his shirt and stepped away, breathless.

"I'm so glad you forgive me, Ali. I don't know if I could live without you."

"It took bullets flying at me to be brave enough to tell you how I felt."

"Let's hope we don't need to go through that again," Blake said.

A grin split my face as tears streamed down my cheeks. "I do have one request."

"Anything."

"You get to tell Grace we weren't really married." When she knew the truth, she would shower Blake with praise, but the first few seconds might be tense.

"I have a feeling I would rather deal with flying bullets, but I'll do it," Blake said, then kissed me again.

About the Author

Sharolyn Richards graduated with a B.A. from BYU-Idaho in English, emphasis in Creative Writing, and with her M.S. in Literature and Writing from Utah State University. The only reason it wasn't an MA was because she didn't want to try to test out of a language so many years after completing her Bachelor's degree. Sharolyn has been published in a nonfiction essay anthology entitled *Wanderlust: a collection of travel tales. Betrayed in Taiwan* is her second novel. Her debut novel, *Arlington's Treasure,* is available in major book stores. When she is not writing or teaching college classes, she likes to spend time with her husband and three kids, cook yummy food, and have dance parties in the kitchen with her kids. She currently resides in Utah. You can find Sharolyn online at sharolyrichardswriter.com and on Instagram @sharolynrichards_writer.

Milton Keynes UK
Ingram Content Group UK Ltd.
UKHW021555230824
447235UK00011B/387